D1235992

Text set in Garamond.

ISBN 1-4515-9165-9

MIRIAM WENGER-LANDIS

GIRL
IN
MOTION

A NOVEL

Chapter 1

I am a dancer from the beginning. At two years old, I walk across our kitchen floor in Rock Island on my pointes. At ten, I read every ballet book I can get my hands on, and my ballet teacher is the most important person in my life besides my mom and dad. At thirteen, I spend every day after school at ballet class, picturing princesses, swans, and tutus. At sixteen, I am accepted to the School of Ballet New York, and by now I know I am going to be a professional.

The School of Ballet New York, better known as SBNY, is the feeder for Ballet New York, the now-legendary company Nicholas Roizman founded in 1948. SBNY is the most exclusive and renowned ballet school in the country, and thousands of hopeful dancers try out every year. The school picks only two hundred out of thousands for the summer program from their national audition tour.

My mom drives me to Davenport to try out for the SBNY summer course, right after I turn sixteen. They barely have us dance; they just ask us to point our feet and lift our legs. Madame Sivenko runs the audition, an intimidating woman in her sixties who is the head of the school. She is more interested in if we have the raw material than if we can actually dance.

I look the part, and when the acceptance letter comes, the head of the Rock Island Ballet School tells me I am the first girl from Rock Island to get into SBNY in the last ten years. I read about, romanticized, and dreamed of SBNY since I was a little girl, but I don't know if I thought I'd ever get in, much less go there.

My mom surprises me with her enthusiasm. "Well, Anna Linado, it looks like you're going to New York for the summer," she says with a hint of regret in her voice after I showed her the letter. My parents never ask me if I want to go, they just assume I do, and they are right. There is no question in my mind that ballet is my destiny.

My stomach turns over when the cab crosses the Queensboro Bridge and I see the skyscrapers for the first time. I've read about New York and seen it in movies and on television for so many years. I'm nervous, filled with anticipation, and excited too. The SBNY summer course is a six week audition, and the school only asks a handful of students back for the full academic year. I'm going to be one of them.

This gets me thinking. In Rock Island, I was the girl with the best body and the most potential, but at SBNY, everyone will have been the top student back home. I'll be no different from the next girl. We all lose some of our edge by coming here, but the ones who last turn into razor blades.

The SBNY and BNY studios have been the center of the dance world for decades, and there will be tension in the air the minute I step off the elevators on the fifth floor. The Roizman building, located in of one of the tallest high rises at Lincoln Center, represents both a legend and a creative force. There will be hopeful, intense faces of young girls rushing off to class with hair in tight buns, and mothers, whispering to each other in the waiting areas about pointe shoe prices and potential. Staff members will do their best to slip by unnoticed, which is impossible, since hopes and dreams will forever be desperately tied to them.

Victor Caldwell is the king of the empire. He's the artistic director of Ballet New York. The board appointed him the year Nicholas Roizman died, but who would want to follow a legend? Victor Caldwell was a long-time principal with BNY before he took over the company.

I know that BNY has pushed forward in an effort not to become a museum, or a sad imitation of its glorious past, but from everything I've read, the decades following Roizman's death have been an unavoidable disappointment. All Victor Caldwell and Ballet New York can really do is move forward and look towards the future. I know that SBNY is not just any ballet school, it's *the* ballet school. And the future of ballet begins in the same place that all futures begin: with the students. Us. Me.

I'm an only child and was the only serious ballet student in my small town. Now, all of a sudden, I'm surrounded by kids just like me from all over the country and abroad. It's exciting and scary at the same time. We're housed in the most beautiful dorm in Manhattan, right at

Lincoln Center on the Upper West Side, only two blocks away from Central Park. The dorm feels new, with blue carpeting and pictures of BNY dancers on the walls. My floor is girls only, and the bathroom is communal and located near the elevator.

"Welcome to the School of Ballet New York," Madame Sivenko announces before she takes roll the first day of the summer session. Vivienne Lalane, another teacher who is younger and prettier but no less intimidating, stands silently behind her, looking each of us over. Next to Vivienne is Simon Saunders, one of the most famous ballet teachers in the world. He has white hair and a kind face. I'm surprised he's so ordinary-looking, for a man who personally coached, mentored, and groomed the best dancers in the world.

My class, the second level from the top, is a group of the skinniest girls I've ever seen, and it bothers me that it's hard to tell us apart in our black leotards, pink tights, and tight buns. Everyone's eyes shine with excitement.

We have class five days a week, three classes a day, and I quickly forget about being homesick. The classes emphasize ballet, mostly technique and pointe, but we also have jazz, modern, *pas de deux*, and Pilates. It's the best summer of my life. All I have to do is dance, have fun, and fall even more in love with ballet.

All the summer students live in the dorms, and Kristen Green, my roommate, becomes my closest friend. She's from Florida, and has brown hair, long legs, and a beautiful smile. We're in the same class, and we go to the

Statue of Liberty, the Empire State Building, and the
Metropolitan Museum of Art together. She's at least six
inches taller than me; I'm one of the shortest in the
program and she's one of the tallest. Kristen talks about
Jeff, her boyfriend at home, all the time.

"Jeff loved me even after I got my wisdom teeth
out," Kristen says one night after we've crawled in bed
and turned the light out. "We grew up together in
Clearwater. I don't remember not knowing him. To be
honest, I just want to dance with our local ballet company
when I graduate high school. I know I'm only sixteen, but
he's the one, Anna."

"That's so romantic." I picture Kristen and Jeff
getting married, having kids, and spending their weekends
barbecuing with their parents, and it's so opposite from
my plans. She doesn't have any long-term interest in
New York or in a serious ballet career. Kristen came
because her ballet school and her parents convinced her
she couldn't throw away the opportunity, but I don't
think she realizes what a big deal it is to get into SBNY.

I like Kristen and getting to know other kids my
age, and being around the famous teachers. Madame
Sivenko is from Russia, danced with the Ballet Russe, and
by now is known more by her name than by anything she
ever danced. After three husbands, all now dead, her life
is about ballet and the school. I'm fascinated by her, but
she terrifies me.

After class one day, I overhear Madame Sivenko talking to a nervous mother in the hallway. "They're only here for a few weeks, we can't invest a great deal in these students," Madame Sivenko says. "This is an audition for our year round program. We only accept about five from the three hundred here for the summer."

"I understand that," the mother says, "But some of them get in, and I'm counting on my daughter being one of them, so I have a lot of questions. What do the year round students do about academics?" she asks.

Madame Sivenko looks her up and down. "Our boarding students generally attend Young Artist's High—YAH—on West 60th Street," she says. "The school is designed for dancers, actors, and musicians with professional schedules, and it's very accommodating. A few do correspondence, which means they earn their GED by completing their coursework by mail. The students must focus primarily on their SBNY classes. For a dancer to succeed, ballet must be everything."

"Ballet must be everything," the mother echoes. "Nearly every famous American dancer has been a student here. My daughter is very talented, as I'm sure you've noticed, and—"

"Excuse me," Madame Sivenko says, sidestepping the conversation. She walks away to teach her next class. Her disappearance down the hall re-emphasizes how many ballet mothers she fends off, and I wonder how I'm ever going to impress her. I obsess about how high the standards are, how tough it is to get in, how rigorous it is to stay, and how even after beating out competition all across the country, most of us are still ordinary.

New York is filled with dance legends. Baryshnikov takes men's class at SBNY, Gelsey Kirkland walks in as I walk out of the New York Library of the Performing Arts, and the current star of BNY, Diana Rampling, buys toilet paper and nail polish at Rite Aid. I stand in the line behind her with the same shade of nail polish in my hand. Diana is in town because of an injury. The rest of the dancers, along with Victor Caldwell, are in upstate New York for their summer residency.

The students are so focused on dancing that I start to notice our personalities fade into the background. The classes are very impersonal, and I never get the feeling the teachers know much about any of us. Sometimes I wonder if they even know our names. Even to each other we quickly become bodies and competition most of the time. I try my best not to compare myself too much with the other girls, but it's hard not to.

Hilary Marshall has red hair and freckles, a pale, good-looking girl, with an upturned nose. She's in the top class, one level above Kristen and me, and pretty in a notice-me way. She wears a lot of makeup, and she's barrel-chested, about five foot eight. Hilary seems to know she's going to be a principal dancer. The teachers are always correcting her when I look in.

Corrections demonstrate potential, and favoritism. A criticism is a positive event in our world and even sought after in class, no matter how harsh. It's always better to be criticized than to be ignored. I stand in the doorway of the SBNY advanced class, watching, my heart sinking as I worry that I'm never going to be as good as these girls. The advanced class in Rock Island barely compares to the lowest level here.

Some students get drunk and high every night, and my impression is that drugs and alcohol provide an escape from imperfections and a way to fit in. There are many students with eating disorders, and the weirdest part is that a lot of people seem proud of it. It's like a skinny body is an accomplishment.

The people at SBNY are nothing like the people I knew in Rock Island. Everyone at ballet school is intense. I miss Rachel Silverstein, my best friend, but she would be so out of place, just because she's friendly, outgoing, and likes to have lots of hobbies. I think peer pressure more than anything encourages us to ignore everything but ballet, but I'm okay with it. I know it's probably not healthy, but I'm more comfortable in this environment than I ever was at home.

Kylie Underwood, a girl from Texas, gets sent home halfway through the summer because her roommate catches her stealing money and clothes. I can't believe anyone with the opportunity to come to SBNY would throw it away. I have friends back home who would kill for her spot. They never would have done anything so stupid. I don't think it's about who wants to succeed though. It's about who they choose.

The summer races past, and by the second to last week they've already asked four people back. When I hear Hilary is the fifth, I lock myself in a bathroom stall and cry my eyes out. I'm not even sure I'm going to be tall enough for BNY. All the dancers in the corps are at least five foot five, and I'm only five foot two. I'm scared. I have no idea what's going to happen to me, and no control.

"Phone for you," Kristen says after lunch when we're back up in our room before the second class of the day. It's the last week of the program. My dad is on the line, and I hurry to the phone. "Not going out to the street to call him back?" she asks.

"I'll just take it here this one time." I hate having private conversations in the dorms, where everyone is always spying on everyone else.

I put the phone to my ear. "Is everything okay?" Why is he calling in the middle of the day? I hope Mom isn't sick again. Dad is usually busy at work until late in the evening.

"We just got a call from Madame Sivenko," Dad says.

I feel my heart stop.

"Honey?" my mom says, coming on the line. "Dad was home for lunch today, and it was the strangest thing, the phone rang and we stared at it—"

"You got a call from *Madame Sivenko*?"

My mom starts to laugh.

"You've been invited back for the year," Dad says.

I can't help it, I scream. I scream and laugh and then start to cry.

"Oh sweetie, we know you've been dreaming of this your whole life," Mom says. "We're so proud."

"Does that mean I can move here for real?" I ask. I'm only sixteen, and I'm not sure I'm ready to leave home for good.

"Would it stop you if we said no?" Mom asks.

"We want you to be happy," says Dad. "I don't know how we'll afford it, but if it's what you want—"

"I have to come." I'm so scared my skin starts to tingle.

"You know, Anna, there's only one good job in ballet," Dad says. "The prima ballerina job with Ballet New York. Who's the star? Stacy Hannah, right?"

"Its Diana Rampling now, Stacy Hannah is retired." I know all about them because I study my *Dance Magazine* like the Bible. Diana Rampling is probably the most famous ballerina still dancing today, and Stacy Hannah and her partnership with William Mason are legend; Stacy was the star of BNY for over twenty years.

"Well, I guess you'll be next," Dad says.

"I can't believe they asked me back for the year!" It doesn't seem like something that happens for real, to anyone I know, much less to me. "I can't believe it! I'm going to be a student at the top ballet school in the entire county—the entire world. This is the most amazing thing that has ever happened to me, *ever.* I love you guys! I love you! I love you! I love you! I'm gonna make it—just wait and see. I'm gonna get into Ballet New York. I'm gonna make it."

And I mean it. I've never felt anything so passionately in my life.

I spend two weeks at home after the summer course, trying to pack my life into two duffle bags. Rachel, my best friend since kindergarten, hangs out at my house almost every night and helps me pack. She doesn't understand why I'm leaving home.

"I can't believe you're going to miss junior prom," she says, twirling her blonde ponytail. Rachel never understood my ballet obsession during junior high and high school, while she played tennis, joined the cheerleading squad, participated in student government, and lost her virginity. The way I see it, her life is about friends and having fun. We've talked on the phone and hung out at each other's houses a few times a week for as long as I can remember.

"Who would I go with?" I ask. I've never had a real boyfriend. My clearest memory of school is of me rushing away with my hair in a bun.

She studies her body in my full-length mirror. We're physical opposites: she's tall, curvy, athletic, and I'm small and shaped like a stick. "Oh Anna, we'd find someone," Rachel says. "You're pretty—*hello.*"

I feel a rush of love for her. I don't relate to guys our age, and she doesn't understand, but that's why I'm leaving, isn't it?

"Dinner! Come to the table!" Mom calls up the stairs. She's been making all my favorite meals lately. I love my family and friends for the small things—it's the small things that make my heart feel heavy more than anything right now.

While I love the comfort of home, my friends, and my home, I can't wait to be surrounded by people who get me. It's such a relief, because the ballet world is something you have to experience to fully understand.

Chapter 2

I force myself to close Gelsey Kirkland's autobiography, *Dancing On My Grave,* when the plane touches down at JFK. It's about her life as a prima ballerina, her drug addictions, love affairs, legendary partnership with Baryshnikov, and of course, her eventual ruin. I think it's funny that Dad thought it would convince me not to become a dancer. I can't stop reading.

I'm sweating by the time I drag my three duffel bags outside the airport and get into a cab going to Lincoln Center. I watch the skyscrapers fill the skyline, and feel more excited than ever to be back.

There are a few people crowded around the front desk on the 14th floor of the Roizman building, so it takes about twenty minutes to get the key to my dorm room. The RA working behind the desk—a dark-haired girl with a nametag that says Nicole Ashbury—looks me up and down.

"Hi." I smile, wanting to bond with her. "Anna Linado."

"Oh," Nicole Ashbury says. "Hi." She has sharp gray eyes, carefully lined in black, and she's beautiful. Later I learn that Nicole is a native New Yorker and has been at the school since she was nine, but in the moment, all I know is how small town I feel next to her. She riffles through a stack of envelopes. "You're on the fifteenth floor. Here's your key."

"What's my roommates' name?" I ask as I take the envelope.

"One sec," she says, checking another list. "You're with Hilary Marshall. She's new too."

"Hilary from the summer course?" My heart sinks.

"Yeah, I guess," Nicole says. "Most of us already picked roommates last year, so that's usually how it goes."

"Okay," I say, dismayed. Hilary was never friendly to me last summer, and on some level I dislike Nicole for giving me the news. "Nice to meet you."

"Yeah," Nicole says. She runs a hand through her long silky hair and I notice the gleaming emerald ring and two diamond-studded bracelets on her left hand.

I collect my stuff, feeling Nicole's eyes on me, evaluating.

I take the elevator up two floors to my room, which is at the end of the hall. I walk towards it wondering what I'm doing here. I don't feel worthy of this place; it feels unfamiliar, intimidating, and cold, even though I lived in a different room here last summer. When it was temporary it didn't scare me half as much.

Hilary is already in the room unpacking when I open the door. She looks up, and I'm surprised by how happy she looks to see me. There are two twin beds on opposite sides of the room, two desks, two dressers, and two closets.

"You're here!" she says. "I hope you don't mind, I already took the bed away from the door, but I left you the newer desk. Can you believe we're roommates?"

"I know," I say, trying to match her enthusiasm, and immediately second-guessing all my earlier impressions. "That's fine about the beds. Are you so excited to be here?"

She pulls her long red hair over one shoulder and crosses her arms, leaning back against her bed and examining me. The pause makes me nervous. I can't help noticing how long and thin her legs are, even in jeans.

"They've been begging me to come for a long time," Hilary says. "This was my third summer. They just better put me in Advanced. I'm going to be so pissed if they put me in the second to highest level just because this is my first full year."

"Oh," I say, wishing I felt that confident.

"Are you going to Young Artists High?" she asks.

"Yes. You?"

"Please, I'm doing correspondence," she says. "I don't have time for school, really. I'm here for dance." Hilary is from Pittsburgh, and I've heard that most of the major ballet schools have been drooling over her for years.

I turn away from her and start to unpack, losing myself in the security of organizing my life. My stuff looks out of context here. I do my best to make the room feel like home. Hilary brought her own TV, which she generously sets up in the middle of the room so we both can watch. She finishes unpacking long before me and leaves to go explore. I can't help noticing how expensive her stuff looks. I'm grateful to have the room to myself for awhile. It feels weird to share a room with a stranger.

Eventually I lose interest in unpacking and sit down in the window ledge. I can look straight down onto the plaza, far below, and beyond it I can see the Metropolitan Opera House and a corner of the New York State Theater. It makes me feel very small.

Hilary and I go down to dinner in the school cafeteria together. I'm glad to have her so I'm not alone, even though we aren't that comfortable together yet.

"I hope the food isn't as disgusting as it was last summer," Hilary says, charging ahead of me into the cafeteria. I stop to gather silverware and napkins, taking a deep breath as she moves away.

"You're new," someone says behind me. I look up into a pair of blue eyes.

"I'm Tyler Hoffman," he says. He has dimples and dark curly hair. I notice he's about five foot nine and growing, feet too big for his body, wide shoulders, and scrawny but well proportioned. I think he's beautiful.

"Hi," I manage, intimidated. "I'm Anna Linado." I admire his confidence.

"Well," Tyler says, "welcome to New York, Anna."

I watch him head past me towards the food. He walks like a duck.

"You can sit with me," Tyler says over his shoulder. "But I hate girls that don't eat."

"I eat." I've been asked if I'm anorexic many times, but honestly, I don't know what the line is between normal eating and what I do. My mom refills my plate mid-meal, but I always feel guilty about eating. How could I not? I think needing food is a sign of weakness and a path to career destruction. To my ballet teachers there's no such thing as skinny, because we could *always* stand to be skinnier.

Hilary is pouring milk into two bowls of cereal, and I stop and whisper to her, "We're going to sit with the guy in the blue shirt, ok?"

She whips her head around to look at him and I cringe. "Cute," she says.

I walk away to fix a plate with small portions of pasta and broccoli. Hilary meets me at the cashier's line, and we walk out into the dining area together. She follows me over to Tyler's table. He's sitting with two guys.

"This is Anna," Tyler says to the others. He's sitting on the end, and I take the seat across from him. "She's new."

"This is my roommate, Hilary," I say. "She's new too."

"Not so new," Hilary says, taking the odd seat, but leaning forward across me to talk to everyone. "I've been here three summers in a row."

"I'm Charlie McAdams," says the boy next to me. I lean back so he and Hilary can wave at each other, noticing that he's skinny with curly blonde hair. "And this is Jesse Ferguson," he says, tilting his head to indicate the good-looking guy across from him. "We're just discussing if Simon will be back from Royal Danish in time to teach our first class Monday. We have that BNY soloist Jeff Talroy the rest of the week. If he doesn't like me I'll die."

"Jeff Talroy is awesome," Jesse says, biting into a chicken leg.

"He's mine, bitch," Charlie says. He kicks Jesse under the table.

Jesse kicks him back before biting into his hamburger. I start to realize how cute he is, but when he catches me staring at him, I can only meet his gaze for a few seconds before I feel my face heat up. He looks more like a football player than a ballet dancer, with light brown hair, a broad chest, and ripped arms on full display, thanks to his white tank top.

"Jesse and Charlie are both second-years," Tyler says, directing the comment to me.

"Oh," I say, making eye contact with Tyler. "Cool."

"So is Madame Sivenko a bitch or what?" Hilary says to the whole table.

Jesse snorts, and Tyler raises his eyebrow. I get the feeling they like her.

"Let's get real," Hilary says. "I want to know all the school secrets."

"She's a bitch on wheels," Charlie says. Hilary smiles at him like he's her old friend, and I'm reminded of

Rachel, back home in Rock Island, who could always draw people in with one look.

I'm quiet the rest of the meal, nervous that I'll say something stupid. They gossip freely about the teachers and returning students, and I wonder if I'll ever feel comfortable and included enough to do the same. I still feel like an outsider looking in.

Ballet classes begin two days later. School doesn't start until next week, so I spend an hour doing and redoing my hair, hoping I'll look as perfect as possible. I get it wet, pull it into a tight ponytail, twist it into a figure eight, clip it to my head, and jam in bobby pin after bobby pin until my scalp starts to bleed. When it looks perfect from all angles, I spray everything down with hairspray. I apply mascara, sand-colored lipstick, and powder. I put on my new black leotard with velvet straps, my pink tights, my grey knit legwarmer pants, my purple ballet sweater, and my black bedroom slippers. Hilary is ready in half the time, and she leaves to go downstairs and warm up long before I'm ready. Before I leave the room, I stand in front of the mirror, willing myself to be good. I'm frustrated that after all this effort, I still don't look quite right. I don't know why.

Our class assignments have been posted in the waiting area on the fifth floor, outside the studios. There are two levels in the girls upper division and 30 students in each class. I'm disappointed to see I'm in the lower class, as is Hilary, which I doubt she's happy about. It's only my first year, and even though Hilary is in the lower class too, it's hard not to feel disappointed. Most girls in the higher class were here last year, but there are two new girls that went straight to the upper level. Every decision—even every glance—from a teacher or student seems to carry deep significance about my future as a dancer. I sigh and decide it's okay, as long as I make it to the upper class by next year.

Hilary is already standing by the door of the studio when I walk in, studying her reflection in the mirror. She'll probably always beat me here—I'll have to get up before her to go to school. I feel a tinge of jealousy. If she does work on her correspondence courses in the morning, she won't even have to leave our room.

"Hi," I say, passing Hilary.

"Mmph," she says. She looks over my head at her reflection, grabbing her heel and stretching one leg up next to her ear as she holds on to the *barre*. When she lets go of her foot, her leg drops an inch. She runs her hand over her face and curses, then smoothes her red hair back into her bun, never taking her eyes off herself. I walk across the room to claim a *barre* spot on the other side, willing myself to be confident and hating that Hilary makes me feel insecure.

Barre spots on the first day are crucial. Dancers are territorial, and after the first day we'll always stand in the same place. It's like that everywhere. I stake my position out carefully: I don't want to be too conspicuous, but I make sure I stand in front of a skinny mirror with an unobstructed view of my reflection.

The room starts to fill up. I notice the returning students are much louder than the new ones, catching up with each other after being away the entire summer. I sit down to put on my shoes. I'm nervous for this class, afraid I'll be the worst and the school will decide they made a mistake about me. I miss the familiarity of my studio back home.

The girl who takes the spot in front of me at the *barre* is petite, thin, with blonde hair and high cheekbones. She glances over and we make eye contact.

"Hi," I say, feeling the urge to make friends. "I'm Anna Linado."

"Marie Damoulin," she says with a French accent, rolling the *r*. She sits down in the frog position, knees bent and flat against the floor, soles of her feet touching. We smile and then go back to preparing for class. I stretch out in the middle splits and start to pick my fingernails, wondering if she thought I was too forward. Marie shoves her legs into the floor, cringing as she forces the position.

Vivienne Lalane, the teacher, walks into the room wearing a green leotard, black leggings, a black skirt, and pointe shoes. She's in her fifties, but I think she has a body like a twenty-year old, and every muscle on her looks like a knife slash. She was a principal with Ballet New York when Roizman was alive. I think her class is analytical, and liked her a lot over the summer, even though she's sort of overly obsessed with the process and the day-to-day mechanics of dancing. A correct *tendu* is still life-or-death to her, even after so many years. From what I can tell, Vivienne was a subtle and introspective dancer, qualities reflected in her teaching.

At ten o'clock on the dot, Vivienne claps her hands three times. All twenty-five of us stand ready and loaded with nervous tension. I notice that except for Marie standing next to me, I'm the shortest in the class. In my state of total insecurity, I read the expression on Vivienne's face to mean she's thinking about all the other bodies she's taught over the years, and how few of them actually made it anywhere. She walks to the *barre* and shows the first *plié* combination, and even though I watch closely, in my terror I miss the sequence. I put my left hand on the *barre* along with all the other girls and follow. I take comfort that every other girl in the room seems to radiate a certain level of fear. My heels touch in first position as I struggle to elongate my muscles. I hear the music begin.

I bend my knees as deep as I can, keeping my heels on the floor. When I straighten my legs back up, I strain to feel the resistance between my muscles and gravity. The third time I bend my legs, my heels release as I go all the way down to a full knee bend. As I come up I feel my inner thighs spiral outward like eggbeaters, my stomach tightens, and I bend forward over my straightened legs to touch my nose to my knees. I inhale, bringing my head back up, and at the end of the phrase of music, I arch back with my right arm over my head. It's a struggle to make my body do these unnatural movements, although I've been working on making them natural for as long as I can remember. Even still, every time I start I feel like I'm swimming against a current.

We all point our right foot to the side and put it back down a foot's length of space away from our left foot. Vivienne circles the room, examining us, lost in the shape of our bodies and looking hard for ways to make us more perfect. We repeat the same series of *pliés* in second position. It feels better as we go and my muscles begin to feel warmer.

Hilary walks front center as soon as we put the *barres* away, and she stays there, in the first group, the entire class. It's cheeky and the returning students exchange glances. Nicole Ashbury, who I've heard was the star of the class last year, stands right next to Hilary, sometimes too close. I think Nicole looks ready to smack her, but Hilary appears oblivious. Hilary is a shade taller than Nicole, and Nicole has longer legs, but otherwise they have similar bodies. They're both good for different reasons: Hilary fits all their physical criteria, but Nicole knows the style and what the teachers want.

There's a lot of competitive energy in the room. We all evaluate each other, but Hilary and Nicole come across as the most aggressive, and I stay as far away from them as possible.

It feels good to dance even with all the nervous tension, or maybe even more so because of it. I focus on perfecting each and every second of my movements rather than gaining attention, because I don't feel ready to be noticed. It's safer to go in the second line of the second group and be inconspicuous. Marie stands in the front line of the second group. I notice she doesn't need to be pushy to be noticed; her looks help her stand out. I feel comfortable dancing near her because our body types are similar. She's good, very controlled, and serious. As the class progresses and I have more time to get comfortable, I start to feel like I belong. I'm not the best but not the worst either.

Our bodies grow warmer as Vivienne puts us through the paces: *tendu,* small leg movements pointing our feet on the floor and finding our balance on one leg, *adagio*, slow, strength-building combinations requiring high extension, *pirouettes,* turns away from the standing leg and towards the standing leg, *petit allegro*, combinations with small jumps and fast footwork, and *grand allegro*, big jumps across the floor.

"What are you *saving* it for?" Vivienne shouts, and I like the way she pushes us to try harder as we leap across the floor. The class is simple yet challenging to me, and her corrections are brutally honest. I try to read Vivienne's expressions, which are intense, but her face isn't easy to read. She only seems to comment when she wants improvement.

At the end, we gather to show our appreciation. I extend my right arm over my head and point my right foot behind me. My right hand comes to my heart as I kneel, and I bow my head in a *grande reverence*, feeling that dancing is a privilege. I'm so happy to be here. I love when class is over and I'm hot, sweaty, and tired. I feel like I'm accomplishing something, even though improvement in ballet is so gradual. There's no concrete proof anything positive has happened in one class, but sometimes, like today, I can *feel* myself changing, and I'm sure I must be getting somewhere.

When I glance up, I see a shadow in the doorway and feel a chill run down my spine. Every pair of eyes in the room darts to our new audience, Victor Caldwell, the artistic director, in the flesh. I feel awed by the sight of him, and think he's an imposing man: tall, handsome, and severe. I'm guessing he stopped by the school for a meeting and decided to peek in. My first glimpse of Victor Caldwell fills me with desperation. I know why I'm here, but when I see him I feel I have to get in to BNY, or I'll *die*.

"Class dismissed," says Vivienne.

We applaud politely, and disband to pick up our bags and clear the studio. Victor Caldwell turns abruptly and walks down the hall. I feel so unsatisfied, like I haven't started anything yet.

I'm overwhelmed by the academic expectations at Young Artist's High. The school manages to accommodate our hectic dance schedule, but in return they expect academic excellence. Without YAH a real high school diploma would be impossible. Dance is a full time commitment, and at this level we don't have time for normal life.

The school is five blocks away from SBNY on West 60th Street. When the weather is nice I love the moments outside, but by December, I'm miserable running back and forth in the cold and snow. Marie swears in French all the way there and back. It's excruciating for me to go from a zero degree snowstorm to doing *pliés* in my leotards and tights. There's no time to warm up, and it's against the dress code to wear leg warmers or sweaters in class. I know it's because the teachers need to see every inch of our bodies, but it's miserable all the same.

At home in Rock Island I warmed up for thirty minutes before ballet, but now there's only a half an hour between my morning French lesson and my first ballet class. During that time I run back to SBNY, change my clothes up in my dorm room, take the elevator down to the ballet school, and shove my pointe shoes on. The rush always makes me feel unprepared and crazy. I never wear my hair down for school because I'd lose even more time to stretch before ballet class.

After the year gets underway, we're moving so fast I'm hardly aware of what I'm doing. I come to understand high school isn't a place to meet people, and I talk to the same people at YAH as I do at SBNY. Our classes are small, and my main focus is my career, not academics, not socializing, and not dating. It bothers me a little, but that's just the way it is. The movie actors, models, Broadway stars, and musicians have their own cliques. We don't socialize, and over time I realize I only feel comfortable with dancers.

Hilary and I spend a lot of time together at first. I'm meeting more people than she is because I go to school, but she's the one I brush my teeth next to in the bathroom before bed. I want to like her, and part of me wants to be like her, but sometimes I can't stand her.

One day when I come home to find Nicole hanging out in our room, I'm surprised that she and Hilary have become friends. It happened subtly and I hadn't noticed. I assumed they wouldn't be friends because they're so competitive with each other, but they turn into a twosome as the weeks go by, and I learn not to expect to always be included. I don't mind because I'm not sure I like them that much. I feel kind of ambivalent about being friends, because I don't always like them, especially at ballet. I'm surprised one day when they invite me to go out for frozen yogurt. Maybe because it happens infrequently, I feel happy they're including me.

"Unbelievable," Hilary says at the frozen yogurt stand, "I asked her to put sprinkles at the bottom of the cup. Sprinkles. Not sprink-le. How can I go on under these conditions?" She puts her hand against her forehead. "Where do they find these people?"

"That's where the dolly-dinkle dancers end up working," Nicole says. She snaps her fingers and walks on ahead of us. "You could be sprinkling someone's sprinkles someday too." Hilary walks faster to catch up to

Nicole, and I hurry after them. Their legs are longer than mine, so I always seem to be walking a few feet behind.

"I'm sure you'll show me how it's done," Hilary says to Nicole.

"But just think of all the free frozen yogurt," I say.

"Nicole will just puke it up," Hilary says.

"Shut up, Hilary," Nicole says.

"Why would anyone puke up free frozen yogurt?" I ask, trying to joke off something I think might be more serious than it sounds. They laugh, and it makes me feel good. I like when we can play around together. They're never like this at ballet.

During the first few months, the teachers explain the details of the Roizman style at length. We stand and listen as much as we dance. As much as I want to believe I'm learning the true Roizman philosophy, I think the teachers remember him according to their individual experience, and put their own spin on everything. Sometimes I love them for their interpretations, but I don't think that what we're getting will never be 100% *it*. The degree of separation frustrates me.

I'm the most guarded with Madame Sivenko, who is almost two decades older than Vivienne. She danced for Roizman in the early days, when he was more focused on his individual dancers than on inventing new technical tricks. She's threatening because I feel like she judges us on our personality. I feel safer with Vivienne because she's obsessed with technique, which isn't as personal. Simon focuses only on the basics and repetition, and he makes me feel like I'm not even there. Some days I like being ignored, because it feels like I can do anything and it won't matter, but other days I feel angry that he doesn't say anything. No matter who the teacher is, I feel like the history here haunts us in every class.

The combinations Madame Sivenko gives are complicated and sometimes impossible, but she's most concerned with how we look doing nothing. "You look like you're all asleep back there," she says to the second group standing in the back. "The wall is more interesting."

One day when Madame Sivenko is telling a story, I leave my spot at the *barre* and walk closer to her because I can't hear. She spins around, eyes narrowing. "You," she points at me, "are too forward."

Embarrassed, I nod and slowly back up to my spot at the *barre*,. Madame Sivenko spends the rest of the class going out of her way to shred my self-confidence. She criticizes everything about me: my hairstyle, the angle of my chin, how fast I turn, where I focus my eyes. Even though I usually like corrections, I feel attacked. It seems like she's punishing me for showing too much interest, and for being myself. I have a hard time not taking it personally.

The next class, Madame Sivenko attacks Faye Poelson, a quiet, unassuming girl with brown hair who has talent but sloppy technique. "Could you *bother* to pointe your foot?" Madame Sivenko screams in Faye's face, seemingly out of nowhere. Faye winces, visibly shrinking an inch. I notice she hides in the back of the room the rest of class. I'd rather not see Faye hurting because I like her, but it makes me feel better. Madame Sivenko's personal vendettas seem less personal to me over time after I see that I'm not the only one she likes to torture.

Vivienne is my favorite teacher. She's tall and intimidating but seems much more human, and I find it comforting that she has a husband and kids. I think it's glamorous that Madame Sivenko is still single, but she's not as sympathetic towards us, and she always seems wrapped up in one rich boyfriend or another.

I love the intensity Vivienne brings to class. "Don't act," Vivienne says, pacing in front of the class. "Just dance. And whatever you do, don't think." I turn the command over and over in my mind, wondering how to apply it. I have to think to be able to dance, but my movements should be one with my thoughts, not one before the other.

I forget a lot of what Madame Sivenko says, but Vivienne's corrections stick in my head, even in other classes. My thoughts wander the most in Simon's class, because he's mysterious and almost always silent. His class is almost like meditating, and I feel like he emphasizes clarity and simplicity by not saying a word. I feel so lucky to be in his presence. During my first class with him he says only one sentence, "The basics are essential and nearly impossible to master." I can barely hear his whisper of a voice, but it isn't his voice that's important to me, or what I take away. Simon's essence seems like more than enough to guide me, and in his class, I eventually start to feel like I can hear my own inner voice.

A month into the school year, I walk into the studio for morning class and Hilary is standing in my spot at the *barre* behind Marie. I stop in the middle of the room, feeling a surge of anger. There she is, stretching, examining herself in the mirror, smoothing her red hair back into her bun.

Marie looks over at me as if to say, "Sorry, she just took it, I didn't know what to do." The other girls are watching too, and I feel them waiting for a scene. Nicole's eyes are all over me. I can sense her amusement. Hilary ignores all of us to study her reflection.

I know I should stand somewhere else and act like I don't care. But if I take Hilary's usual spot, I'll have to stand right at the front of the room, by the door. If I try to stand somewhere else, I'll take another person's spot. I get that it's some sort of joke, like when she kept messing up my carefully alphabetized CDs, but it's just not funny to me.

Madame Sivenko walks in the room, and the last thing I want her to see is that I've been bullied. I march over next to Hilary and squeeze in between her and Marie, pretending as if Hilary isn't there. I shove my pointe shoes on and tie the ribbons as fast as I can, as the class is already beginning. I sense Hilary's surprise and irritation, but I'm determined to ignore her as much as she's ignoring me. Hilary holds her ground and I hold mine all the way through the *barre*, even though we end up kicking each other during every exercise. Madame Sivenko sees us dancing on top of each other. She pauses, amused, and doesn't say a word.

From that day on, it's impossible for me to think of Hilary without gritting my teeth in anger. It takes two weeks for us to start speaking after the incident, and I'm the one who makes the effort first. She seems to feel like she won some sort of power struggle, but at least she doesn't take my *barre* spot again.

My feet hurt all the time, in and out of pointe shoes. SBNY doesn't allow ballet slippers in the upper division. The dancers in Ballet New York wear pointe shoes all day, every day, and we have to learn to do it too. By the end of the day the pain is so excruciating I can barely walk. My feet alternate between numb and on fire, and shooting daggers of pain race up my legs. I wonder if I'll be crippled in my old age.

At my old ballet school I wore pointe shoes for two hours a day, at most, but here the shoes are on between four and six hours. I try to hide my suffering as I struggle through it, and at least while I'm dancing I can usually forget. My true feelings creep out before class, when I have to shove my cold feet into the shoes, and at the end, when I take them off and remember what I'm doing. I work hard to smile in front of the teachers, because that's what's expected. We're a parade of smiles.

Marie takes her shoes off next to me at the end of Madame Sivenko's pointe class and the right foot of her tights is caked with blood and pus. She grimaces, and I look from her face to her foot back to her face, seeing the tears rise in her eyes.

"That looks horrible," I say.

She glances at me. "I want to die."

"Cut it off."

"Ha ha," she says. "You are so helpful."

"I try."

"Who would have thought you were so sarcastic?" she says, snapping her pointe shoe ribbons at me. I raise my arms in defense. "I am far too important in the world to spare a toe," she says. "This foot could be worth millions. Have a little respect."

"Of course," I say. "What was I thinking?"

"I have no idea," she says, shaking her head. She hobbles out of the studio.

My toes have formed blisters too—my feet bleed all the time. I stare off into space for a while after Marie leaves, wondering how I'll reach the point where this all seems natural. It would be great if I didn't have to wear any lamb's wool or padding in my pointe shoes, so I could put them on as easily as sneakers. The more my feet and my body hurt the more determined I am.

Hilary's solution to her foot pain involves soaking her feet in a bucket of ice water at night. Every time she puts her feet in the freezing pail she wails and yelps, looking for sympathy. I sit sewing pointe shoes at my desk, generally ignoring her in favor of the ritual of preparing a new pair of shoes. She doesn't like to be ignored.

I think about the pain in my feet as little as possible, but I think about my pointe shoes all the time. Everyone has their own rituals with their shoes, and my routine comforts me. First, I cut the satin off of the tips of the shoes to expose the canvas and prevent slipping, and then I darn the edges to keep the material from fraying and to give it a neat appearance. Second, I sew a thick strip of elastic to go over the arch of my foot, attaching to the heel of the shoe to keep it on while I'm dancing. Third, I sew one long ribbon to each side of the shoe, which I'll cross over the front of my arch, circle around my ankle once, and tie in a knot. The ribbon is cosmetic—it doesn't really help keep the shoe on as well as the elastic. Fourth, I bend the stiff arches to make them more pliable to dance in, and then I slam the box of the shoe in the door hinge to soften it. Finally, to help them last a bit longer, I put an entire bottle of superglue inside the tip of each shoe, spray a thin coat of shellac along the shank, and stand the pair upright against the radiator to dry.

One night, I try to wear an old pair of pointe shoes to bed to see if it will help me get used to them.

"You're a psycho," Hilary says, watching me.

"I know," I say, feeling brave. "It's just an experiment." Later that night, I wake up screaming and rip the shoes from my feet. It hurts. It hurts *like hell.*

All foot pain aside, my body's inadequacy bothers me more than any pair of pointe shoes. Physical pain is nothing compared to the mental anguish. When I do get a correction in class, I have a hard time sustaining the change for more than a few minutes. There's so much to think about. There are countless times when my body does the very thing the teacher said was incorrect, against my own will.

"You can't be this stupid," Madame Sivenko says after I mess up the *petit allegro* right in front of her. She makes me repeat it alone without music while everyone else watches. "How can you let your rear stick out like that?" she says when I'm finished. "No wonder you can't get off the ground." Her words cut me.

I hide in the shower, sobbing, at the end of the day. I feel like I'm going to pass out from the steam, the physical suffering, and most of all, the humiliation of having all my flaws observed and pointed out over and over again.

If our first class of the day ends a minute early, we peek in at the end of Advanced Men. Watching men's class, it strikes me as ironic that ballerinas have a powerful image and male dancers are viewed as effeminate, because the ballet world gives men much more power than women, or at least it seems that way to me. There are fewer guys, they're not as competitive, the technical demands on them are less, their natural bodies are more accepted, and they're outnumbered by women and therefore in much higher demand.

My real thrill at men's class is watching Tyler Hoffman. He's a child prodigy, and the most talented male dancer in the school. His body is long and lean but also muscular, but it isn't just all his physical gifts that make him so special. I think Tyler has individuality, flair, style, presence—a quality of indescribable charm. He's the kind of person who seems like everyone's best friend. The teachers always make him stand in the front, and I *love* to watch him dance.

Charlie McAdams is average height, flexible, and skinny, but he's awkward and his mannerisms are feminine. He's also a drama queen, and because of it he draws a lot of attention to himself whenever he makes a mistake, rolling his eyes, stomping off the floor. "I'm such a loser!" he says over and over. The way Charlie watches the teachers correct Tyler makes me feel uncomfortable. He looks so jealous.

Ling Qi is Chinese, average height and weight, and overly polite. He's quiet and solid which unfortunately, makes him somewhat easy to overlook. I think he's sweet and always seems grateful to be here, but no one ever talks to him, and I can't help feeling a little sorry for him because he seems so socially isolated. He used to do martial arts and has a great jump. When Simon corrects him he looks like he's so grateful he might cry.

Then there's Jamal Jamison, who acts like he's a rap star. Initially I thought he came across as a real tough guy, but the more I know him the sweeter and more entertaining he seems, even though his macho act gets old fast. He's the tallest and already a fully developed man. His skin is dark, he has brown eyes, and he's not very classical. Marie is friends with him, or should I say, Marie goes out of her way to flirt with him, which I find fun to watch, because it's the only time either of them comes across as insecure.

I think Jesse Ferguson is hot. He's close to six feet tall and not a bad dancer, but not great—his jumps and turns are passable at best. It bothers me the way his eyes constantly dart to the door to see who might be watching him, even though he tends to hang in the back. Its funny how outside of ballet Jesse comes across as totally confident, but in the studio he acts like he hates himself.

One day when I'm watching Advanced Men's, the jump combination ends and the music stops. Tyler lingers in front and bends his knees with his right foot pressed in front of his left foot. His right toes point to his right and his left toes point to his left. He jumps up and spins around twice in the air with his legs tightly crossed, landing in the same starting position he took off from. His double *tour en l'air* is flawless. He smiles, enjoying himself.

The others examine themselves in the mirror. Simon is teaching, leaning on the piano and studying his students. Tyler looks to him for a reaction and Simon makes a small gesture with his hand, indicating that Tyler should bring his heels forward as he rotates his hips. Simon hasn't given him approval, but Tyler nods, knowing that the correction is a compliment. Tyler is only fifteen, but it's so obvious they're grooming him for a big future with BNY. Boys that talented are so rare. I'm as enraptured as everyone else when Tyler moves like silk off the floor. He's lost in that zone where he's dancing and all that matters are the steps.

Chapter 3

When the company is in season, the ballet is free for students, and the school likes us to go to as many company performances as we can. They want us to watch the professionals at work. The dancers in the company are only a few years older than us.

At Ballet New York's opening night gala, my ticket is right next to Tyler, which makes me nervous.

"You know, you should really wipe the drool off your mouth," Tyler leans over and whispers in the middle of the first ballet. I ignore him.

"No seriously, stop drooling. You know you're better than those girls," he whispers a few minutes later. I blink.

"Don't make me tickle you just to get a reaction," he tries a third time, and this time, I grin.

"You're really rude to talk during the ballet," I say when the curtain falls.

"You're really rude to ignore me," he says. "Now tell me what you thought. Did you see Pamela Davies fall out of line in the third movement? They should fire her."

We end up talking straight through both intermissions. With Tyler, once the dam has opened I can't shut up. Halfway through the evening I realize there's so much to say we can't seem to stop interrupting each other.

From then on we fall into a pattern of going to the ballet together during the week. Hilary invites herself along once, but it's obvious she's the third wheel, even though she tries hard to charm Tyler. After that, it's understood Tyler and I go alone, which makes me happy, but also drives a deeper wedge between Hilary and me. I can tell it bothers her that anyone would like me more than they like her.

There are many Roizman ballets that I don't know and could never have seen in Rock Island, but now, when I sit in the audience for a BNY performance, it's like I have a new identity and a clearer purpose in life. Every show is both pleasure and research for my future career. Victor Caldwell always slips into his seat in the house just as the lights go down, and I always find myself staring at him.

"I swear he looked at you," Tyler always whispers.

"I think he had something in his eye," I say.

Afterwards, if I don't have too much homework, I hang out in Tyler's room for a while. Sometimes I help him with his homework too. He shuts his door when I come over, which is against the rules since I'm visiting, but it doesn't seem to matter. He lives a flight below me on the guys' floor, which is always dirtier than the girls'. All the guys get their own rooms because there are fewer of them. Tyler never makes his bed and his room is always messy.

"You're so funny," Tyler says to me, lying flat on his back on the floor in his room. "You think every performance is good. It was obvious Diana Rampling had an off night."

"She was beautiful," I insist, sitting cross-legged on the bed.

"You're too nice," he says. Tyler seems to know everything about ballet by osmosis. He's been at the center of the dance world since he hit puberty. Because I grew up far away from New York, I always read ballet books, and it feels like I know it from the outside and he knows it from the inside. "My sister is a sucker, just like you," he says. His sister took ballet first, which is why he got into it. She quit after he came to SBNY.

He watches me from his position on the floor, stretching his arms out to the side. After kicking off his shoes he flexes his feet. His body is long and lean, and I can't help it, I love watching him stretch.

"Why did your parents let you leave home so early?"

"They hardly noticed," he says. "They were busy getting divorced after my dad cheated, with his secretary, no less." He props himself up on his elbow and holds my gaze.

"Wow." I'm not sure how to respond. I thought my family was more screwed up than anyone's.

"I'm going to be the star of Ballet New York," he says. "Then my dad will be sorry. He has no idea who I am." He lays down again, folds his hands behind his head, and stares up at the ceiling.

I consider crawling down on the floor and putting my arms around him, but Tyler seems untouchable, like something beautiful to be looked at only on a stage.

There's a bubble around him that always stops me from trying to get closer.

Marie and I start talking before class while we put our pointe shoes on. She hates Hilary, which fascinates me, but makes me uncomfortable because I still try to think of Hilary as my friend. Or maybe I just feel disloyal since I'm her roommate.

"Hilary is so stupid," Marie says. "Why does Madame Sivenko like her? I can't deal with it today. And why should I make my feet bleed before eleven in the morning?" Marie came all the way from France to get into BNY. I know she cares a lot more than she lets on.

Even though Marie is pretty and has amazing feet, she isn't the best in the class. I watch her a lot since we stand next to each other at *barre*. Her technique is good, but her face always looks tense when we come to the center. I like her personality a lot—she's surprising and funny.

"Tours is near the Loire," Marie says, talking about home. "You know. South of Paris." I don't know anything about France, but I nod anyway. Her parents are very strict and don't have much money. They sold their house and took an apartment to make it possible for her to come to SBNY.

"Why didn't you go to ballet school in Paris?"

"The Paris Opera is fine," she says, "but I wanted to study the Roizman style. I saw Ballet New York on tour in Paris when I was thirteen. After that I knew I had to come here." She licks her fingers and smoothes the wispies back into her blonde twist as she checks her reflection.

"Fine? The Paris Opera Ballet is fine?"

"Don't be so provincial," she says with a smile, but I can tell she's serious.

"Don't be such a snob," I say back.

"My family loves the arts," she says defensively. "The French respect ballet much more than Americans. We bend nature to man. That is why France has so many beautiful gardens and incredible architecture. You Americans lets nature run wild. Just look at all your national parks."

"Whatever." I stand up to stretch my leg on the *barre*.

This makes me think: is nature meant to be tamed? There's a part of me that wants to run wild and free, be an artist unleashed, but there's another part of me that wants to tame and control that impulse. I guess that's why I like ballet—it's the perfect combination of outer structure and inner force. We have to be so disciplined. For example: my back has a natural tendency to sway. I have to figure out from the inside how to shape it back into the standard straight spine that's required for proper ballet lines. But it feels so good to let my back sway, and it's so easy and relaxing to let things go and be as they naturally are. It's not beautiful though. Not ballet beautiful. Not perfection.

Vivienne claps her hands for us to begin.

We go to see *Elements*, a ballet in three acts that I've read about and seen pictures of since I was little. I read the program and Tyler studies the audience while we wait for the performance to begin. I look over at him, sitting straight in his chair, tugging absentmindedly on his jacket as he scans the crowd. He finally looks at me.

"Why does *Elements* only have three sections: *Earth*, *Wind*, and *Fire*? What happened to *Water*?" I ask.

"When Roizman was choreographing *Elements*, the ballerina he planned to make *Water* for got pregnant," he says. "He was so pissed he cut the entire ballet."

My eyes grow wide. "Whoa."

He shrugs and turns to watch the conductor walk up to the stand.

The lights go down and we clap along with the audience as the curtain goes up. A corps of ten girls in long gold tutus dances *Earth*. Their bodies move identically through the same steps.

I experience it almost without breathing, listening with my eyes and focusing my mental energy. The choreography is beautiful. I'm so interested in the dancers; I imagine how they feel at each moment in the performance, what they're thinking about, why they do certain things well or why other things don't have an impact. They work so hard to translate their intentions into perfect execution. My favorite dancers are the most self-aware.

Two and a half hours later the performance is over. We stand and stretch our backs, waiting for the patrons to file out. I notice Hilary sitting with Nicole and Jesse on the other side of the orchestra section. She hadn't mentioned to me she was coming when I was getting ready to leave, and I'm surprised to see her. Jesse looks bored, like he doesn't want to be there. Hilary, in a tight green dress, her red hair loose, is talking loudly on one side of him, and Nicole is on Jesse's other side, looking bored and older in a skirt and jacket.

When they stand up Hilary puts her arms around Jesse's neck and whispers in his ear. Nicole confidently grabs his other hand and pulls him down the row, with Hilary trailing behind. Tyler and I walk out of the theater on the other side, and we wave when we pass them outside where they've huddled in a group. They barely nod at us, but I see a flicker of irritation in Hilary's eyes, and I wonder why things have become so strained between us. Tyler rolls his eyes behind their backs as we walk away.

We pass the fountain on our way home. It looks beautiful lit up at night, very romantic, and with all the courage I can muster I take Tyler's arm. He glances down at me but doesn't protest.

"*Fire* was amazing," I say. Diana Rampling and Richard Jackson were the leads, and it was the kind of performance you could tell they enjoyed—it was obvious they were taking risks and having fun, but also thinking. Diana Rampling was beautiful: tall, long flexible limbs, dark hair, amazing feet. Richard Jackson was masculine and known for his strong partnering skills. "The *pas de deux* was the highlight of the evening."

"Yeah," he says, but I'm having trouble reading him as usual.

Watching the company makes me more determined. I have to be a dancer. Almost every member of BNY went through the school, and now they earn their living dancing Roizman ballets. Those ballets wouldn't exist without dancers to do the steps. Even after thousands of classes, I'm still amazed that a human body can dance *Fire*.

"Do you think I'm going to be tall enough for BNY?" I ask nervously.

Tyler stops and looks at me. I meet his eyes, looking for an answer there, but there isn't one. "Shh," he says. "Anna, you're always worrying so much. Stop worrying and try to enjoy." He wraps me in a warm hug, and my heart fills with happiness.

After a minute he pulls away. "You know, we should dance *Fire* together," he says. The thought gives me a thrill.

"Nicole, let me see your double *pirouette*," says Vivienne. She narrows her eyes and I can almost see Nicole light up under her scrutiny. There's something about the actual moment of being corrected that brings a dancer more clearly into focus. A teacher's notice makes us more *real*. Since we can't speak in class, our only power comes to us passively, by receiving.

"Don't over-cross your *passé*," Vivienne says as she walks towards Nicole in the front line. Nicole is one of her favorites, if only because her non-existent hips, long legs, and pin-shaped head are the ideal Roizman shape.

I wonder if I over-cross my *passé*, and why Vivienne doesn't correct me more. Sometimes I don't know what's worse, criticism or disinterest. I worry that I'm invisible.

Vivienne examines Nicole's starting position for the turn. Nicole angles her shoulders and hips at a diagonal in relation to the mirror, nervous but also pleased at the attention. She puts her left leg directly in front of the center of her torso and lunges forward onto it, her right leg stretching straight behind her, in line with her spine. Both her legs rotate outward from her hips. It makes her toes point away from each other flat to the side. She looks over her hand and stretches her right arm out in front of her nose. Her left arm stretches out to the side, parallel to the floor.

"Right. Go ahead," Vivienne says. Nicole pushes off onto her pointe shoe and rotates to the right. Simultaneously her right leg comes up to form a triangle shape by connecting her right foot with her left knee. As she turns, she leaves her face as long as she can and focuses on her own eyes in the mirror. Immediately she whips her head around and looks back at her eyes again. After two revolutions she stumbles out of the turn.

Hilary moves a little closer to Nicole and crosses her arms.

"Tighten your stomach and pull into a higher *passé*," Vivienne says, ignoring everyone but Nicole. She crosses her arms and waits for Nicole to readjust. Her insistence sends the message that it's not okay to give up. I don't think Vivienne wants us to think we can quit until we do it right, and she knows Nicole never has to try very hard because it comes so easily to her.

I study the twenty-four other girls in black leotards, pink tights, and pointe shoes in the reflection. We look so much alike with our hair in buns. Everyone studies Nicole as if her body is a science experiment, and I wonder if it's wrong of me to think of us as humans at all. In here we're machines.

Nicole places her right foot higher on her left knee and sucks in her stomach as she turns again. Her torso leans too far to the right. She falls off her left leg after the second turn. The *pirouette* is even worse—most of the girls in Children's Division could do better.

"Come on. Spot faster," says Vivienne. I wonder if she thinks like I do that Nicole takes what she has for granted. "That better not be what you plan to do onstage. I shouldn't pay sixty-five dollars for a ticket to see a lousy *pirouette*."

My calves begin to cramp. I feel like we're wasting time, but all of a sudden, Nicole spirals up and hits her center of balance. She whips her head around and turns once. Twice. Three. Four. Five. Six times. At the end she hangs in the air a little. When she finally comes off *pointe* she still has perfect control. Even the finish is beautiful. Nicole smiles.

I've never seen a girl do six *pirouettes*. It's so beautiful it takes my breath away, but it tears me up inside. As much as I love good ballet, when I see something better than what I'm capable of I want to scream.

Hilary immediately begins practicing her *pirouettes* on the side. She whips off a perfect triple, but Vivienne doesn't see it. Hilary looks frustrated.

"The turn was better," Vivienne says to Nicole, "but you didn't listen." I can't help thinking that Nicole got by on luck rather than technique. "I only asked for a double *pirouette*. If I were Victor Caldwell, why would I want to hire someone who ignores my instructions? I could never trust you onstage. Your job is to perform the choreography. That's it." She walks back to the front and claps her hands. The first group takes their places to try again.

I stand in the back and wonder what I'm doing here. If our teacher doesn't even appreciate it when Nicole does six *pirouettes*, how will she ever think I'm good? I can barely do three. If all it took for us to succeed was the ability to do a double *pirouette* when Victor Caldwell asked, we'd all be in Ballet New York.

When we get out Jesse is drinking at the water fountain. "Hi ladies," he says, smiling as Nicole and Hilary stop to give him a hug before they walk down the hall. I wait until they move out of the way before I stop to take a drink.

The cold water feels good on my throat, and I drink and drink until my stomach starts to cramp. When I come up I turn right into Jesse's chest as he's waiting to get another drink of water. He towers over me. "Sorry." I back up and bump into the water fountain.

"How come you never say hi to me?" Jesse asks.

"Hi." My face heats up and I wonder why he's singled me out like this. For the most part we always ignore each other. I thought it was mutually understood.

"That's it?" he asks, with a grin.

I shrug, back away without answering, and then I turn and walk quickly down the hall. I hate being put on the spot like this. It makes me nervous and edgy when he stands this close. He's too attractive. I don't like how cocky he acts either; he's a perfect example of a good-looking guy in ballet who assumes he can have whatever he wants because he always gets it. I wish he didn't feel like he had to charm me. I'd like him more if he wasn't always putting on a show.

I walk into the cafeteria to get lunch before I run back to school. The cafeteria makes me paranoid because everyone is always obsessing over food. I still try to eat three meals a day, but I feel guilty about it. My friends eat much less. I could be skinnier if I tried harder.

I get in line behind Nicole, who's standing with her mom. They're talking and don't notice me. I've seen her mom around a few other times, because Nicole is the only girl in the dorms whose family actually lives in Manhattan. Her parents live on the Upper East Side. I think she lives in the dorms because her parents are rich and agreed to it, and she wanted to have the same experience as the rest of the upper division students.

"God I'm fat," Nicole says. Her mom looks just like her: tall, small head, elegant neck. She's beautiful.

"That's not true," Nicole's mom says.

"What do you know?" Nicole asks. She turns to stare at the French fries. Her expression sinks into the zoned-out look she has a lot of the time when she's dancing.

"Excuse me," I say, reaching to take bun for my veggie burger.

"Oh," Nicole says, looking at me in surprise. "I didn't see you."

"Hi there," Nicole's mom says. "Are you in Nic's class?"

I nod.

"Mom, this is Anna," Nicole says, introducing us. "She's Hilary's roommate."

"Nice to meet you," her mom says, and I shake her hand. "I always like to meet Nicole's friends."

"Shut up, Mom," Nicole says. I'm surprised and bothered by her rudeness, and Nicole's mom looks embarrassed.

"You should have seen Nicole in class today," I say. "She did some great *pirouettes*."

"Really?" Nicole's mom asks. "How nice of you to say. Nicole, you didn't tell me you had such a good class."

"I didn't," Nicole snaps.

"Well then, nice to meet you," I say as I back away and turn to go to the cash register, feeling uncomfortable. I pay for my lunch, and head outside to walk back to school. Nicole has issues. I miss my mom.

Pas de deux class is the highlight of the week. It always makes me look forward to Fridays because it's so much fun to practice dancing with the guys. Jeff Talroy, who's a soloist with BNY, is the teacher. He's from Alabama, has a Southern accent, and seems to like working with students. I think he's cute. He's tall with brown hair and dimples. Plus his technique is incredible.

Jeff uses me to demonstrate because I'm short. I probably get more attention from him than from the other teachers on all the days of the week combined, which makes me like him. I can identify with him more than Vivienne, Madame Sivenko, or Simon because he's closer to our age.

After Jeff sets the combination with me, I alternate dancing with Tyler and Qi. Both of them are good partners. Charlie asks me to go, but I do my best to avoid him because he has awkward timing and digs his thumbs into my ribs. I always want to go with Tyler—all the girls compete for him or Jesse. Marie dances with Jamal. They get along, even though when he does talk it seems like all he says is "yo," followed by swear words. Nicole and Hilary always dance with Jesse. If someone else dances with him, they stand on the side and glare.

"Your turns very nice," Qi says after we walk off the floor after the first combination. He smiles and pats me on the shoulder. I like Qi but he hardly says anything. I wonder if he's as lonely as I am.

"Thanks," I say, as Tyler grabs my hand to repeat the combination with him. We step forward and I let him lead me into the opening *arabesque promenade.*

"Come on, Jesse," Hilary says, dancing on our left, "Eight turns." Jesse exerts more energy into rotating her waist, and as we're dancing I can feel the tension coming off them. They're getting too close to us and she's frustrated that he's not doing what she wants. She always seems frustrated.

"We have room," Tyler whispers, but Hilary dances even closer to me. As she opens her leg out into *arabesque* her pointe shoe slams into my face.

"Aagh." I fall off pointe and step away from Tyler, bringing my hands to my nose. Hilary tries to keep dancing, but Jesse lets go of her. Blood starts seeping out into my palms. The music peters out and everyone moves closer to see what happened.

"It's your fault," Hilary says. "You shouldn't have been dancing on top of me." The other girls look at her, surprised.

"But you—" I start to say.

"You're bleeding," interrupts Tyler. I think he feels responsible, but it's not his fault. I keep my hands pressed against my nose as he touches my wrist. My face starts to ache.

"Someone get ice," Jeff commands. Hilary just stands there.

"I'll do it," Jesse says kindly. He shakes his head as he walks out of the room.

"Thanks, Jesse," Jeff says, turning to me. "Are you okay?" he asks.

"Yeah, I'll just step out for a minute," I say, feeling embarrassed. Jeff guides me to the door, and class resumes as I walk out into the hall. I'm so sick of Hilary and her attitude, her aggressiveness, and her ambition. But most of all I'm sick of how no one ever calls her on her bad behavior.

Jesse meets me with an icepack on my way to the bathroom.

"Thanks," I say, walking past him. "I'm fine." But my whole face throbs.

"No you're not," he says, following me right into the girl's bathroom. I splash water on my face, and then he helps me tip my head back and holds the ice to my nose. I can only stand the cold for a minute before I push him away. When I glance in the mirror I see a bruise already forming.

"Hilary is evil," Jesse says.

I try not to smile. "I thought she was your friend."

"She's a bitch and everyone knows it," he says. "Come on, I know she's your roommate, but it's not like she's a friend of yours."

"How would you know?" I say. "I can't believe you said that." I'm shocked, but also pleased.

"You know, even with a bloody nose, you're pretty," he says. He reaches over and smoothes a loose piece of my hair back into my bun. Why does he get to be so confident? His fingers brush the back of my ear before his hand falls away. A shot of electricity races through me.

"What are you doing?" Is he flirting with me?

"Nothing," he says with a smile.

"We should get back." Our eyes meet in the mirror, but I quickly turn away and walk out. He follows me but I charge down the hall ahead of him.

"Anna," he calls.

"I'm not one of your groupies," I say over my shoulder. I don't trust him.

I open the door and slip back into the studio, but I stand in the back the rest of the class. Dancing doesn't seem like much fun today, even though Tyler keeps coming over and trying to make me feel better. I'm mad at Hilary, but I feel like I have to make peace since we're roommates.

"Thanks," Jeff says to Jesse when he comes back in the room.

"Sure," Jesse says, and I think he seems pleased to get the credit.

Nicole takes Jesse's hand and leads him onto the floor. "You're such a nice guy," Nicole whispers as they start to dance. Jeff watches them carefully, stopping to correct them at the end of the combination. Nicole and Jesse seem to glow under the attention.

Tyler leans against the *barre* next to me. "We look better," he whispers, nudging my shoulder. I feel a rush of affection for him, and manage a small smile.

Chapter 4

On a Sunday morning in late November, I'm sitting on the ground in a corner of the plaza at Lincoln Center. It's cold outside, but I need privacy. I was one of the only girls in my class not hired by a school in New Jersey for their production of *Nutcracker*, and I'm devastated. The New Jersey school uses SBNY students every year, and the production is a big deal—it's a chance to perform in a semi-professional production, a tradition for the upper levels, and a status symbol.

Jen, one of the Advanced girls, comes walking across the plaza, apparently on her way back from church. She's about five foot six; the perfect height, with long legs and a narrow torso. Her auburn hair is pulled into a tight ponytail, and there's a sunken look in her cheeks and around her eyes. We've never spoken before, but I've known who she is for a long time. She looks at me curiously.

"Why are you crying?" she stops to ask.

"I'm not crying," I say. "Don't worry about it."

"It's okay," Jen says, and she seems to actually care. "What's wrong?" She rubs her arms, hugging herself to keep warm.

"It's nothing." I feel like Jen wouldn't understand. She's in the top class.

"Of course. It's nothing." She rolls her eyes, and her exasperation makes me more willing to warm up to her. "Sucks to cry over nothing. Most of the stuff they put us through isn't worth it." She sits on the ground next to me, even though she's wearing nice clothes.

"I didn't get picked for *Nutcracker*."

"Oh," she says. "I get it. But so what? It's just *Nutcracker*."

"It isn't just that," I say, "It's not getting picked."

"If it makes you feel any better," Jen says, "I didn't get in last year when I was new and in your level." A group of Juilliard students walks past us across the plaza, laughing and joking. They seem so self-assured.

"I don't believe it." I'm so surprised. I don't know her personally, but I've seen her around the school for months and she's practically perfect. Maybe none of us are the image we project.

"Why?" she asks. "Because I'm in it this year? I served my time to get where I am now."

She's trying to make me feel better, which is nice, even though I don't really believe it's about serving time. It's obvious who the most talented dancers are, and the best ones are so lucky. I think the teachers love them even if they don't try. It seems to me they don't even work hard, and they still get away with skipping class or throwing attitude. SBNY loves them even more if they seem not to care. I feel like I'm in class every day working my ass off, but they're the ones getting the attention. I'm sick of Nicole's million *pirouettes* and Hilary's amazing extension and Marie's drop-dead gorgeousness. *Sick* of it. I used to be the freakishly talented girl back in Rock

Island. I'm not anymore, not next to the kind of talent they find all over the world to bring to New York.

"It doesn't happen overnight," Jen says, and I start to feel like she might get it more than I'd given her credit for. "Everyone here has problems, we're just experts at hiding the pain. That *Nutcracker* isn't even affiliated with SBNY. Who cares if they didn't pick you? Do you want to make it? You'll cry your way through worse disappointments." The wind whips her auburn hair across her face, and she pulls her scarf tighter around her neck and looks at me.

"I know," I say, but I don't. I pull my knees up towards my chest and hug my legs. We sit for a while. The quiet gives me space to think. There's so much I don't understand, and I feel lost. "This is too is hard."

"Everything worthwhile is hard," she says.

"That's true," I say, and I when I think about it, I actually feel better. She seems nice. Why did I think she was a snob? "You know, Jen, you look different with your hair down. You almost look like a different person. In the studio—"

"Oh, we're all just bodies in there," she says.

We do all look pretty much the same. They've weeded out so many people so that only the ones left have bodies that fit the mold: short torsos, long legs, pin-shaped heads, swan-like necks, flexible limbs, pretty faces, and thin—thinner than thin. We're all so confused about whether we're bodies or machines, but in reality, we're flesh and blood young women still growing and changing.

"Don't worry," she says. "They probably think you haven't picked up enough of the style yet. It's not the end of the world. You just got here."

"I guess," I say, and feel like she wants to be my friend. I haven't felt anything so nice else since I got here. "Thanks."

"Have you ever been to a Broadway show?" she asks.

"No."

"Well, no wonder you're glum," she says. "There are a lot of good things to do in New York—that I could never do back home in Indiana—and the best part is they have nothing to do with ballet. Are you free next weekend?"

"Yeah," I say, feeling suddenly excited.

"Great," she says. "I never have anyone to do this kind of stuff with. Toko is my roommate, and she's nice, but she doesn't speak English. My roommate from last year had the nerve to get a job in Miami."

"Wow, good for her," I say, thinking that Jen really has a lot more experience than I realized.

"Seriously," she says. "Well, we're totally going to hang out. You can't spend too much time moping around like this. It's bad for you."

"I know." How can she read me so well?

"I have to fail a math take-home test," she says. She squeezes my arm before she stands up. "Next weekend. We'll get half-price tickets in Times Square and see something that makes us cry."

"That sounds great," I say, and realize I have something good to look forward to for the first time in months. It makes me smile.

Jen glides off towards the building, and I sit on the plaza and imagine my life in a different way. I'm tired of thinking that all that matters is getting in. Ballet isn't the only thing in the world. I don't know why I think my feelings don't matter, or why I feel obligated to be miserable so much of the time. I'm ready to start having fun.

I work up the nerve to knock on Tyler's door, but he doesn't answer. He's definitely in because I hear noise in there, and then I realize he's on the phone.

"I like you a lot too, Jessica," Tyler says. "But this just isn't working. I'm only home during the summer. I can't be the kind of boyfriend you want." My stomach drops.

There's a long silence, and I hold my breath. Tyler never mentioned he had a girlfriend back home. I know I'm eavesdropping, but I can't help myself. This is why I never talk on the phone in the dorms. It's impossible to keep secrets or have privacy.

After awhile, when I realize I can't hear much and might get caught, I back away from his door and tiptoe away, feeling guilty that now I know something about him he didn't want to share. I also feel jealous. I'm surprised he was even trying to have a long-distance girlfriend. Doesn't he realize that everything important in our lives is right here?

I fly home to Rock Island for two weeks in December, right before Christmas. Hanukkah is already over and we don't celebrate Christmas at my parents' house, but it's nice to be home and see everyone, especially the dog, Sammy. Mom is in good spirits and Dad takes an afternoon off. We decide to go ice skating.

"So tell me something," Dad says at the rink, as we lace up our skates. "What's your roommate really like?"

"Why do you ask?" I say, feeling defensive.

"Do you get along?" Mom asks, grabbing onto the edge of the rink to stand up.

"Uh, I guess," I say. "I really love my new friend, Jen. She's already been there for two years, she's a level ahead of me, but we're the same age. She's such an amazing dancer, and she's so funny—we went to see *Phantom of the Opera*, and she's teaching me to play some of the songs on the piano. And have I told you about Marie, the French girl in my class? She seemed cold at first, but I like her more as I get to know her. She's smart. I have another friend, Tyler, who I go to the ballet with all the time. He's such a great dancer. I can tell he's going to be famous."

My parents smile at each other.

"Since when do you play the piano?" Dad asks. I think he seems proud of me, and it makes me feel happy. "You quit piano lessons when you were eight."

"Oh," I say, "Well I need to know a lot about music if I'm going to be a professional dancer. I need to work on my French too. Someday I really want to go to Paris. All the ballet terms are in French. There's so much I need to learn…"

On New Year's I put on a short skirt and a sparkly top and go to my childhood best friend Rachel's house. Her parents go to dinner with my parents, and Rachel and I are both surprised her parents agreed to let her and her brothers have a party. I'm glad I'll get to see the old crowd though. The classmates who do remember me, and bother to ask where I've been, look impressed when I tell them I've been in New York. Rachel is drunk by the time I get there, and after she spends fifteen minutes making a fuss over me, a cute boy drags her off somewhere to make out. I don't mind. I'm happy to be at a party.

"Come on, have a beer," Rachel's younger brother, Tim, says to me, handing me a drink before he goes back to shining his laser pen light into people's eyes. Someone puts another good song on the stereo, and the living room turns into a crowded dance floor.

I hold my beer and stare at a cute boy I remember from English class in junior high, wondering if this is the right occasion to start drinking. I've never had more than a glass of wine at Passover. The cute guy, Seth, has curly brown hair and looks like Tyler. I wonder if he even remembers who I am.

"Hey," Rachel whispers in my ear, making a re-appearance. "Let's dance." She grabs my hand and pulls me into the center of crowd. Rachel starts moving her hips and running her fingers through her hair. The boy she went off with earlier watches her from the sidelines.

"Come on, Anna," Rachel says, taking my hand and twirling me. "You don't have to be a bunhead tonight." I smile and gulp down some beer, wondering if her parents will kill her if they find out she had alcohol at the party. The music pulses and I start to shimmy. My shoulders pick up the beat, and I move my feet from side to side. Rachel mirrors me, and be both put our hips into it, rolling our stomachs and tossing our hair. Out of the corner of my eye, I catch Seth, the cute guy, watching me.

The boy that likes Rachel pushes through the crowd. "You ladies are hot," he says, moving in the middle to dance with both of us. We move faster, mirroring each other, singing the words. All the pent up energy I try to control in ballet class comes out as I spin, dancing, moving my arms. Rachel laughs at me. We hold hands, moving our feet faster.

"I'm tired," I say eventually, and Rachel and her guy slow down too. I wave before I walk off the floor, feeling happy. They start to kiss. I walk around the corner into the kitchen and slam into Seth.

"Whoa, hi," he says, taking my arm to steady me.

"Hi," I say.

"I remember you," he says, "English class." He smiles at the same time a short girl I don't know walks up and puts her arm around him. "This is my girlfriend, Emily," he adds. She looks me up and down.

"Nice to meet you," I say, not minding her. "I'm just on my way out." I wave and head out the door, thinking about how much he reminds me of Tyler, and feeling happy I really don't live here anymore. I walk the two blocks home.

"Did you have fun?" Mom asks. "You're just in time to watch the ball drop. Want some champagne?"

"Sure," I say, following Dad into the kitchen to watch him pop the bottle open.

"Happy New Year," Dick Clark announces in Times Square. We toast in front of the TV, and then I head up to bed, already thinking about getting back to ballet class. I fall asleep with Sammy curled in my arms, dreaming of New York, while the rest of the world is toasting and kissing under the mistletoe.

"You still aren't separating your fingers," Vivienne says to me the first week back in January. "You need to carry your hand as if you have a diamond ring on each finger. What you need is a ball. Get one and hold it during *barre* everyday. Then you'll be aware of your hand."

I take her words to heart, and the first thing I do that day on my way back to YAH is to stop in Rite Aid and buy a small squishy stress ball. I think Vivienne notices when I bring it to her next class, but she never says a word to me about it again, even though I hold that ball all through *barre* in her class every day for four months.

I realize the significance of her lesson many weeks later, in Madame Sivenko's class, when I look in the mirror and realize I'm unconsciously holding my hand in a completely different and beautiful way. I'm in awe that it became natural to me, and I hardly knew it was happening.

In an effort to get schoolwork done, I start waking up an hour earlier before school. The first day of my new schedule, I walk into the bathroom to take a shower at five in the morning and I hear someone vomiting in one of the stalls. It's a disgusting, retching noise. I freeze, not sure what to do, and feel guilty for being there.

I look at the feet in the stall and recognize Nicole's purple flip flops and misshapen toes facing the toilet. I'm horrified, but not all that surprised. The gagging noises continue and I start to feel sick myself, but I don't want to leave and compromise my early start on the day. I walk past the toilets and go into one of the shower stalls, take off my robe, and turn the water on full blast. I try my best to forget what I've seen. When I get out ten minutes later, she's gone.

I try to avoid talking to my parents on the phone in the dorms because there's no privacy, but on my birthday on February tenth I break the rule. I'm in a rush before dinner with Jen and Marie, and Hilary has gone out to run errands, so I just call them from my room.

"Hi Dad." I'm happy to hear his voice.

"Hi Pumpkin. How are you?" he says.

"Fine." I picture him sitting in his reclining chair, glasses on his nose, researching a sermon, and feel a rush of love for him. Sammy must be curled up on the floor by his feet.

"How does it feel to be seventeen?"

"Pretty good."

"Happy birthday," he says. "Did you make a wish?"

"I'm wishing I'll grow three inches." I've been thinking about it a lot lately.

"Why? You're perfect," he says. I think about how he says nice things so much that it doesn't mean anything to me anymore.

"I'm only five-foot three and everyone in the corps of BNY is at least five-foot six. If I've stopped growing I won't get in to BNY no matter how well I dance."

"That seems like a stupid rule," he says, and I'm grateful for his support.

"Everything is about what looks good onstage," I explain. "A short girl in a row of tall girls looks all wrong. The corps has to look uniform."

"So you'll be a principal," he says.

"Dad," I say, feeling frustrated, "everyone starts at the bottom. Even Stacy Hannah did before she became a principal years ago. Diana Rampling spent five years in the corps before she got promoted. That's where we learn how the company works. Someone has to retire or leave to make room for someone else to move up."

"It's like that in every profession," he says, sighing.

But ballet isn't like every profession. I think about how we diet, take laxatives, puke, and obsess over fat grams. Jen doesn't eat anything except cereal. It seems to me that the school outwardly denies encouraging eating disorders because they can't have the liability if we starve to death.

It isn't just weight. Madame Sivenko told Patty Harris, another girl in my class, that her breasts were a distraction, and so Patty Harris had a breast reduction over winter break. I didn't even think her chest was that big, a C-cup, maybe.

"You look so much better," Madame Sivenko told Patty when we started back. I felt like screaming when I heard her say it.

"How's Mom?" I ask now. She usually picks up the phone if she knows it's me. "Is she still volunteering at the hospital?"

"Yes," Dad says. "She's fine. We're thinking about a trip to New York. I'd love to go to the opera. We could come see you."

"No," I say sharply.

"No?" he asks. He sounds hurt.

"You wouldn't understand." I don't want anyone in New York to know that they're not thin and sophisticated. But I can't say that to him.

"I have to go, Dad."

"Bye, Anna," he says. "Have a good birthday. We miss you."

"Me too," I say. "Thanks. Bye, Dad." I hang up and stare blankly out at the traffic on Broadway for a while.

When I walk back inside, I pass by the tiny library and notice Jesse in there, studying. I stop for a minute to watch him, writing furiously and tracing his finger along a line in a textbook. Usually when I see him he's surrounded by girls; I've never seen him alone. His face has an intense, concentrated look. He glances up, and our eyes meet. I feel unnerved by the way he looks at me. It's like he can see all of my fears and insecurities, as easily as I can see his.

Chapter 5

Madame Sivenko pulls me aside after Friday class. "Are you eating?" she asks.

"Me?" I have no idea where this is coming from. The other students stream past me out of the studio. I'm horrified to be singled out by her like this, and for something I didn't even know was an issue.

"We can't have eating disorders in this school," she says. "I'll be weighing you once a week from now on. If you lose too much weight you'll be expelled."

"But I don't have an eating disorder." I feel like I'm going to cry.

"It's no use lying," she says. "Every Friday morning, 9:45 in my office, weigh-ins until the end of the year."

She walks out as I stand there, open-mouthed. I'm shocked. And then I notice Nicole, still sitting in the back of the studio, watching me. I suddenly feel certain Nicole talked to Madame Sivenko, maybe because I caught her puking in the bathroom. I didn't know someone could be this evil. I feel so upset that my whole body starts to tremble, and I hurry out of the room before I say something I might regret.

Audition tours begin in the winter and early spring. The major schools in San Francisco, Seattle, Miami, Boston, and Houston come to SBNY to hold auditions for their six-week summer training programs, and the major companies affiliated with those schools also hold a separate audition. I don't take the company auditions. I don't feel ready yet. I want to finish high school before I join a company, and I plan to spend the summer training hard, so I focus on the school auditions. SBNY doesn't let us stay for the summer session—they need the room to screen new students for next year.

Every week I go in to Madame Sivenko's office for my weigh-in, and every week I'm 95 pounds, so after a month or so it becomes a formality. Counting fat grams is nothing compared to what some other people I know are up to, but there's nothing I can say. They think what they want to think, and as angry as I am, I know I have to let it go.

In March, I get a letter from San Francisco. I sit at my desk after dinner, willing myself to open it. The envelope is thick, so it has to be good news. There's a knock on the door, and Jen bursts in the room before I even say "come in." She's always doing that.

"Did you get it?" she asks.

"This?" I ask, holding up the envelope.

"Open, open," she commands.

"Okay, bossy," I say, ripping it open. "Dear Anna Linado," I read, "we're pleased to inform you that you've been awarded a full scholarship to our summer program in San Francisco—"

"Yippee," Jen says, "me too! Me too!"

"Really?" I stand up and grab her hands. "You have to go! We can party the whole summer—"

Hilary opens the door and walks into the room. "God I can hear you guys shrieking all the way down the hall," she says.

"We're going to San Francisco," I say, happy enough to feel warmly towards her.

"Well I'm sure Jen is," Hilary says. "Did you get in, Anna?"

I feel my heart shrivel up and freeze. "I got a scholarship," I say.

The look on Hilary's face makes it clear she didn't even think I'd get in.

"Where are you going this summer, Hilary?" Jen asks, sensing my anger and trying to diffuse the tension. She's so good at reading me.

Oh, I'm going home to Pittsburgh," Hilary says. "I got a scholarship to San Francisco too, but it makes more sense for me to go home and show the students at my old school what they're working towards." She kicks off her shoes and hops on her bed, stretching her legs out in front of her and staring at herself. "My feet hurt. And my hip hurts. I don't know how I do this," she says.

Jen and exchange a look. "Let's go find Marie," I say. "I want to know if she got into San Francisco too." Jen waves at Hilary and follows me out of the room. We pause in the hallway while I double check to make sure I took my key.

"I can't believe *she* got a scholarship," Hilary says from inside the room, to no one in particular. Jen just looks at me. I feel sick to my stomach. I've tried hard to be friends with Hilary, but we don't connect, and it seems like the more I try to be nice to her, the more it blows up in my face.

Marie is in her room holding her acceptance letter when Jen and I arrive. Her room is straight out of a magazine ad—designer comforter, flowers in the windowsill, expensive perfumes and lotions on a glass tray. I've never had a friend whose parents invest so much money in their child.

"Are we all going to San Francisco?" Marie asks.

"It looks that way," Jen says. "Are you interested in getting an apartment with us?" She studies the dresses hanging in Marie's closet. "Marie, you have the nicest clothes," she murmurs. After a pause, she adds, "My dad has a college friend in San Francisco who I bet would sublet his apartment to us. He and his wife travel every summer. It's right on Van Ness, just a few blocks from school and the War Memorial Opera House."

""I do not know for sure," Marie says. "I am very particular about my space. I have always had a single here—"

"Well you don't want to live in the dorms there, do you?" I ask. "Come on, relax for once. We'll have so much fun. Jen says she knows how to cook."

"I make fat-free pizza," Jen says.

"Ugh," I say, tired of the words. "I'll order in."

"I can make crêpes," Marie says. She tilts her head at us and smiles, warming to the idea. I like getting her to loosen up.

We sit around Marie's room planning for another hour, and by the time I head back to my room to get ready for bed, I'm envisioning the best summer of my life. I'm in such a good mood that when I open the door to my room it takes me a few minutes to process what Hilary did.

The desks and dressers have been moved to create a barrier in the middle of the room, essentially blocking in Hilary's side. She's piled books and extra pointe shoes high on top of the desk shelves to create a wall, and the TV has been turned so it faces her bed, and I can't see it. There's a small opening by the closets for her to squeeze through to get to her side. I stand there in shock for awhile, trying to process what this means. Hilary is not in the room.

I knew we weren't as close as we'd been at the beginning of the year, but I hadn't seen this coming. As I get in my pajamas, I practice all the different things I want to say to her when she comes back. I start to feel confused and tired, so I crawl in bed, turn the lights off, and wait.

Close to midnight, Hilary opens the door, flips the light on, and walks into the room with Nicole, laughing. I sit up. Nicole takes one look at me and spins on her heel and walks out. Hilary walks right past me and squeezes through the opening to her side. I jump out of bed and follow her, overwhelmed by my own anger.

"Don't I get an explanation?" I demand, crossing my arms.

"I don't owe you anything," she says, taking her earrings out. "But if you must know, you annoy me. I'm sick of you pretending we're friends when I know you're jealous. You're a loser and I don't want anything to do with you, so quit acting like we're friends just because I got stuck being your roommate. Now get out of here. You're not allowed on my side."

My mouth falls open as I struggle for words, but I can't think of anything useful to say. "I thought you were my friend," I manage. I feel so betrayed.

"You're such a baby," Hilary says. "I'm not talking to you anymore."

I back away and crawl back into bed, in shock. She turns on the TV, loud, and especially because I can't see the screen, the sideways glow of it bothers me as much as the sound. I start to cry.

"Turn it down," I say, but she ignores me. I put my face in my pillow and sob, feeling so sad I can barely remember why I was happy a few hours ago. It takes hours to fall asleep.

I call home the next morning before school from the payphone outside.

"It's six in the morning," Dad says.

"I hate it here," I say. "I want to come home. Why did you let me do this? The people here are horrible. I hate ballet. My roommate is a bitch. I'm so miserable. Please let me come home." I start to sob and I can't stop. My dad waits, letting me gasp and choke and cry it out.

Finally he says, "Come home then. We'd love it."

"Good. I'm quitting." It feels good to say it.

"Good," he says. "We could use your help with the laundry. Maybe you could even get a job at McDonalds. I'll teach you to mow the lawn."

"Gee, thanks," I say, feeling so frustrated I kick the plastic wall.

"I mean it," Dad says. "You can quit whenever you want."

I burst into a fresh round of sobbing. He waits patiently until I'm finished, and then I hang up and walk to school.

Hilary and I don't speak for almost two months. The school focuses on the annual spring workshop for the top class. Madame Sivenko and Vivienne each stage a Roizman ballet, and a guest choreographer from the company choreographs an original piece. In Rock Island I was always the lead in the spring recital. I'm sad watching all the girls in the class above prepare for the performance. All the guys are in it. I'm happy for Jen, who gets a soloist role, and I try to live vicariously through her.

I'm not the only one who thinks the workshop is a big deal. *The New York Times* always publishes a review. Artistic directors from major companies in the United States (and abroad) fly in for the workshop. SBNY students ready to start their careers have an advantage because of it—they have a second shot after the auditions. Victor Caldwell handpicks his favorites from SBNY; BNY never holds auditions. The other companies sometimes offer a contract after workshop if they find someone they like. At that point, dancers who might have turned a contract down after an audition will reconsider. If Victor Caldwell passes them over, the advanced students have to go elsewhere or quit by the time they graduate high school.

By the time workshop actually happens in late May, after months of watching the upper class rehearse, I can't wait for the year to be over. Marie and I sit together in the audience. The stage reveals things about dancers, and I think it's interesting to watch everyone up there, trying to put everything they've been working towards into a brief, impressive performance. I see qualities in people I hadn't recognized before.

"Next year that will be us," Marie says.

"I hope so," I say, but it seems so far away.

"And then we will get our apprenticeships with BNY," she says confidently.

"If Victor likes us," I whisper. "He didn't even teach our class this year."

"Next year he will," she says.

Victor Caldwell isn't the only artistic director in the audience. William Mason, the director of Los Angeles Ballet Theatre, Charles Diamond, the director of Ballet San Francisco, and Bruce Pollock, the director of National Ballet Theatre, are all in the audience too, representing four of the top companies in the United States. To me they seem like gods.

Jen dances the soloist role in *Afternoon Symphony*. She's calm and often reserved in person, but onstage she's a total extrovert, smiling her heart out. I think her technique is clean, strong, and precise. The role is all jumps, and she breezes through it.

Jesse, Jamal, and Tyler, and one of the top girls in the school, Kaley Press, dance a *pas de quatre* in a new piece by Richard Jackson, one of the BNY principal dancers about to retire. The choreography is nothing groundbreaking, but I think Jesse and Jamal are solid, and Kaley Press and Tyler steal the show. She has long legs and amazing extension, and when they walk on for their pas de deux, the audience gasps at their beauty before they even start to dance. I think Tyler partners Kaley with confidence and grace through slow *developpés* and *promenades*, as she lifts her leg so high it seems to touch her ear, and they execute a difficult press lift, where he holds her over his head in an *arabesque* pose, one leg extended behind her, his arms straight and solid as he walks her around the stage. His stage presence is warm, humble, and attentive to his partner, and I think he makes

Kaley look even better than she does on her own. The applause goes on forever when they finish.

After the last performance, Victor Caldwell goes backstage and offers apprenticeships to Jamal Jamison and Kaley Press. I'm surprised Tyler and Jen have been overlooked, but Tyler is young and doesn't seem concerned. Victor probably doesn't think he's ready yet. Jen also has another year of high school left, but she's devastated. I know the teachers led her to believe that she would get in to the company this year. She's one of the best dancers in the school.

"I asked Madame Sivenko, and she said Victor thinks I have thick legs," Jen says to me over dinner in the cafeteria. "She told me to do something about it over the summer." With that, she pushes her bowl of cereal to the corner of her tray.

"Your legs are not thick," I say, but it doesn't help. I feel bad for her.

"Do you want to room together next year?" she asks.

"Yeah, for sure," I say. "I'd like that." I can't wait to get away from Hilary, and I love Jen.

"I don't know how I'm going to make it through another year here," she says, and I wish so much I knew how to make her feel better.

In the days following the workshop, Jen sinks into a depression and doesn't get out of bed for days. I can't seem to do anything to cheer her up. To add to Jen's misery, Charles Diamond, the director of Ballet San

Francisco, hires one guy and two other girls from the workshop performances. I feel depressed too.

Out of the upper class of twenty-five girls, only five made it into a top tier company. Most of the others will be reevaluating their dreams, just like I might be after next year. I'll die if I don't get into Ballet New York. *Die*.

Our end-of-the-year conferences happen at the beginning of June, when the city is just starting to get hot and humid. A lot of people, like Hilary and Tyler, are going home for the summer to take classes with their old ballet teachers, and the school is getting ready to screen new students over the summer to replace the people who graduated, got jobs, or were expelled.

"They always kick some people out," Marie says. We're eating frozen yogurt on the plaza, racing to finish before it melts everywhere and I have to go in for my conference. I'm trying not to think about how nervous I am. All our afternoon classes are cancelled this last week after workshop.

Madame Sivenko's office door is closed when I go upstairs, so I take a seat in the big leather chairs in the waiting area. It feels odd to wear jeans and a t-shirt at the school instead of a leotard and tights.

The door opens and Hilary comes out. Her red hair is hanging down over her face, but when our eyes meet as she passes me it's obvious she's been crying. "Are you okay?" I surprise myself by asking. I feel a twinge of sympathy for her.

"Leave me alone," she says, and she seems genuinely upset.

"Anna Linado," Madame Sivenko says from inside the office.

Hilary pauses and glances back at the door, and then she fixes her green eyes on me. "They didn't kick me out, if that's what you're wondering. She just told me I was turned in. This school can kiss my ass."

"They think you're turned in?"

"I'm not turned in at all," she says. "And they're going to be sorry."

Her attitude immediately kills my urge to care, and I can't think of anything to say. She spins on her heel and walks away towards the elevators.

My stomach is in knots. I'm not sure I want to know what they think of me. It already takes so much nerve to walk into a room full of mirrors and other dancers every day, and I'm not sure I have any left. I say a few prayers, walk into Madame Sivenko's office, and take a seat looking up over the desk.

Madame Sivenko crosses her arms when I sit down. Her dyed-blonde hair is pulled back in an even tighter bun than usual. Was she really a ballerina back in the day, and did she really have an affair with Roizman? He's like one step away from God.

"Well," she says. "Let's have a look at your file." She opens a manila folder and flips through the papers in it. I study the ballet manuals and videotapes on the shelves, the paintings of dancers on the walls, and the pigeon on the ledge outside the window, trying to disengage from my feelings.

"Anna Linado," she continues. "Vivienne wrote, 'Lots of potential, but not enough improvement.' I agree. You're too comfortable in technical habits from your previous training. I don't feel you have a good grasp of the Roizman style yet."

"Oh," I say, surprised.

"Simon notes you have perfect attendance," she says.

In my defensive state, I take that to basically mean that Simon doesn't even know who I am, even though I've been in his class twice a week for the entire year. Am I really that invisible?

"Well, okay, but I don't have an eating disorder," I insist. "I passed all of my weigh-ins."

She just blinks. There's no way I'm going home to Rock Island next year. Isn't it obvious to her that the only thing that matters in my life, the only thing I truly care about, is this? It's the only thing I have. I've never identified with anything else. I was never the girl that boys liked, the girl that played sports, the girl that was cool, the girl that was young and wild and crazy. All I've ever been is the girl that danced. Without it—I don't know—I'm lost.

"Well, maintain your weight this summer," Madame Sivenko says. "And get stronger on pointe. Perhaps we haven't given it quite enough time." She folds her hands together and rests them on the desk.

My mind is racing. When I do all my homework for school, I always get a good grade. I feel so frustrated that no matter how hard I work at ballet, I might always just be mediocre.

"Go on now," she says. "We'll see you in the fall."

I walk down the hall, disturbed by such vague feedback. How could I have not met their expectations? I was never injured, and never missed a class. Every minute I wasn't dancing, I felt like I thought about how to dance better the next time, and there wasn't one correction the teachers gave me that I didn't try my best to apply. All my confidence feels shot.

Saturday morning, Vivienne teaches my last class of the year. I can't stop obsessing about my conference, and like every dancer who feels like they didn't receive enough praise for all their hard work, I find myself blaming her and glaring in between combinations.

After class, I screw up my courage and walk behind her on the way out the door. "Ms. Lalane, may I speak with you?" It's funny how we call her by her first name behind her back but we would never do it to her face. My voice sounds weird to me. I've never said a word to her in nine months of being in her class every day of the week.

Vivienne raises an eyebrow, making real eye contact with me for the first time ever. "Come on," she says. I follow her down the hallway past Madame

Sivenko's office, nervous. She takes me to the conference room, which is filled with a large mahogany table surrounded by swivel chairs.

"Have a seat," she says. She leans her arm on the table and I sit down. The leather chair is freezing cold. Vivienne looks me over for a minute, letting her brown hair out of the bun into a ponytail. I'm wearing a black leotard, pink tights, and my pointe shoes: our uniform, but suddenly I feel naked.

Vivienne pulls up a chair. She crosses her muscular legs, smoothes her chiffon skirt, and folds her arms. Her face doesn't have a drop of makeup on it, but I think she's attractive and intelligent-looking.

"Well," she says. "I suppose you're here about your conference."

"I wondered what I should do for next year."

"Look," she says. "You didn't grow. The shortest BNY dancers are at least five foot five."

They were disappointed in me because I didn't grow? Why didn't Madame Sivenko say it? "I know." My eyes start to tear up.

"At least we're letting you come back," she says. "Next year, prove you're serious. This is not a place to fool around."

I hate that I'll never be more than another one of the bodies that passes through the school. Why doesn't she have any compassion? She was a dancer once too.

"I'm not here to fool around," I say, determined to make her see me the way I see myself.

"Look, I hope you realize that dancers are disposable," she says. "You might as well take that dream and put it away in a box. Most people can't get a job. The ones who do make it in to a company, even a small one, almost never make it out of the corps. Is that what you want?"

"I just want to dance." As I say it I feel like such a cliché. "It doesn't matter where I get a job."

"Let's be honest. Of course you care which company you dance with. If you didn't you wouldn't have come here. You're too caught up in the romance," she says. "Most dancers in BNY had the natural talent and it happened for them. It's a mistake to want something you aren't suited for. You're only asking for a let down."

"Are you saying I'm not going to make it?" I ask, surprised that she seems so heartless. I guess I wanted to believe she cared about me; it's what kept me going to her class every day. But it doesn't seem like she cares now.

"I watch dancers every day," she says. "I can tell everything about your personality by the way you dance."

She leans forward, puts her elbows on her knees, and looks me right in the eye. "Anna," she says. "I think you like dancing because it feels natural to your body. You have beautiful feet, good proportions, and nice extension, but you may be too short for BNY. Maybe you do feel like you need to dance, but I don't think you fully understand what it means to be a professional dancer."

I fight back tears, feeling stupid and incredibly naive. "I'm not looking for something easy! *I want to do this for real.*"

She leans back in her chair. "I see," she says. I suck my breath in, hoping for a fleeting moment I got through to her. We stare at each other. I open my mouth and then shut it again. I'm not sure what I'm doing here at all.

"Don't ask me to predict the future," she says. "I don't know what's going to happen."

I feel like she's lying. "Fine. Thanks for talking to me." I stand up, angrily wiping away the tears already running down my face. "Next year will be different."

"Good," Vivienne says. She swivels her chair back and forth, looking thoughtful. "Come back ready to work."

I open the door and walk out.

When I'm halfway down the hall, Vivienne calls my name. I'm frustrated, angry, and upset, but I turn around and look at her in the doorway of the conference room. "Anna," she says. "You're right about one thing."

"I am?" I can hear my heart pounding in my ears.

"Talent," she says, "means nothing without desire." She pauses. "Remember that. Talent means nothing without desire."

Goosebumps rise up all over my skin. I turn away and walk to the elevator, turning her words over and over in my mind. Ballet is eating me alive. I want to get into BNY more than anything. I've started to hate myself for wanting it, but after all these years I feel like I'm in too deep to turn away.

Chapter 6

I fly home to Rock Island for a week in June. My mom leaves me alone in my room for the afternoon while she fixes a welcome home dinner. She's left me a stack of newspaper clippings on my desk: articles about the Rock Island Ballet in the local paper, Ballet New York articles in *The New York Times*, articles about osteoporosis, the importance of breast exams, and the benefits of calcium. I glance at them briefly and then throw them all in the trash.

I help set the table for dinner, noticing how hard my mom is trying to make things nice for me. "I wanted to make this visit special," she says.

We sit down to eat the minute Dad comes home. He's obviously tired, but cheerful, how he always is after a full day of work.

Dad bites into a chicken leg. "Great dinner, Sue. Anna, you should come home more often. We haven't had a meal this good in ages."

"Oh David," Mom says, but she smiles.

"Don't get used to it, Dad. I'm off to San Francisco in a couple days."

"We know," Mom says, and I feel like she's sad to see me go.

As much as I love them, I feel like a guest. They had a life together before me, and they have a life together after me, now, too. But, then again, maybe it's my fault for being so eager to leave.

I fly into San Francisco on a Saturday morning. During the flight I play Stravinsky on my headphones and imagine myself nailing six *pirouettes* in the middle of a performance of *Fire*. I'm so caught up in my dancing fantasy that I hardly notice my surroundings and almost miss my luggage on the carousel.

I admire the fog, hills, and pastel houses on the taxi ride to the apartment, and compare it to the skyscrapers and pedestrians in Manhattan. What I want is to find some sign, any sign, of where I belong—which place is *me*? I wonder if Charles Diamond, the artistic director of Ballet San Francisco, will be around, and if he'll see me in a way Victor Caldwell might not.

Our sublet is in a complex on a busy street, and as we pull up, I look at each of the windows and try to picture Jen and Marie inside, going about their lives as aspiring ballerinas. The driver opens the door to nudge me out of the cab. I start, then climb out and pay him. He watches me drag my suitcase towards the door and into elevator before he drives away, seemingly amused by my determination, but unwilling to help. The elevator takes me up to the eighth floor, and I struggle down the hall towards our apartment and knock on the door, excited to see my friends.

"You're here!" Jen says, throwing the door open. She's in jeans and a t-shirt and looks happy, relaxed, and sweet as ever. We hug, excited to see each other.

"I missed you," I say. It feels more like coming home to family than my trip to Rock Island. Marie appears behind Jen, smiling. I feel so relieved to be done living with Hilary.

"We have been waiting for you," Marie says. Her blond hair is down, her face is makeup-free, and I'm surprised that she's wearing jeans too. She almost looks like an ordinary American teenager, except that she's so beautiful she barely looks real.

"Come in," Jen says, grabbing my wrist. "We've been unpacking." I follow them into the apartment, which is small but nicely furnished with a view of the street. Jen and I agree to share the larger bedroom, Marie takes the smaller one, and we all seem happy with the arrangement. When I can't unpack anymore I walk in the living room and start jumping on the sofa.

"This rocks," I say, and remember my first time outside Rock Island's dolly-dinkle ballet school, when six weeks seemed like an eternity to be away from home. I fly in the air from the couch to the sofa chair as Jen walks through the living room to rummage in the kitchen. Now six weeks seems like an eternity to *be* at home.

"We're going to be tourists on the weekends," Jen says. "I promised my parents I'd explore, and not just live in the studio."

"Okay," I say as I flop in the sofa chair. "It's true, we're seventeen and on our own in San Francisco, we shouldn't spend all their time staring in the mirror." But I don't mean it because staring in the mirror is exactly I intend to do. I point my foot in front of me and examine the high arch, already fantasizing about how much I want to improve. Jen, Marie, and I may say we want to be normal, explore, and have fun, but part of the reason we get along so well is because we know deep down that ballet is the priority.

Jen is in the top class in San Francisco, one level above Marie and me, just like it was at SBNY. We don't see the kids staying in the dorms much outside of class, so we spend nearly all our free time together exploring Fisherman's Wharf, Ghirardelli Square, Golden Gate Park, Haight Street, Chinatown, and North Beach.

Marie and Jen didn't know each other as well in New York because Jen wasn't in our class, but now we eat all our meals, walk to and from ballet, hang out at the apartment, and explore the city together. By the second week, we can almost read each other's thoughts. I feel so close to them.

One Saturday, after a long day of wandering around through Golden Gate Park, we go out for dinner at the Hard Rock Café. Marie marches right past the line to get our names in with the hostess, and it reaffirms what I've noticed since we first got here, that she's become much more assertive now that we're not in New York.

"Jen, is she—" I start to ask.

"Yep," Jen says, and she looks embarrassed, "she's flirting with the cute manager, and check it out, we already have a table." Marie gestures at us to follow her, and I grab Jen's arm and follow Marie and the manager to a table by the window.

"This was so nice of you," Marie says, and she touches his arm. The look on the manager's face makes me want to laugh. He knows what she's doing, and doesn't seem to mind.

"You ladies have a good time," he says. "I'll be sure to send over some dessert." He winks at us before he walks away.

"That was disgusting," Jen says. She unfolds her napkin and looks down at her plate, but a blush creeps up her neck.

"Maybe so," I say. "But Marie was working it." I wish I had that effect on men.

"Don't tell me you liked him," Jen says to me, serious. Marie giggles.

"No, but I want to know how Marie suddenly turned into an assertive seductress," I say. "She was never like this before."

"It is simple," Marie says, "I do not have Madame Sivenko and Vivienne around making me feel bad about myself."

"Maybe it's my traditional upbringing," Jen says, "but it doesn't seem appropriate to me to be that forward." She wraps her fleece sweatshirt tighter around herself.

"Why not?" I ask. "Why are we always doing what's appropriate and never having a life? I'm ready to do something crazy. Marie, dare me to do something."

"Well, well, well," Marie says.

"Anna," Jen says, "Please don't make me regret going out in public with you."

Marie leans over and whispers to me, her blonde hair hanging in front of us. I nod, enjoying the look on Jen's face.

"Sounds good," I say.

"What?" Jen asks. "What are you up to?"

"Oh nothing, just eat," Marie says as the food arrives. We fall silent as Jen eats her Caesar salad a small bite at a time, and Marie downs her veggie burger with calculated bites. I cut my chicken into pieces and eat fast. While Jen is still eating, I dig a pen out of my purse, grab a napkin, and stand up.

"I'll be right back," I say.

"Where are you going?" Jen asks.

I walk over to the table next to us. The two middle-aged couples look friendly.

"Excuse me," I say, "my friends and I are taking a short survey. Appropriate to flirt with the manager to get a better table? Yes or no?"

They look at me bewildered for a minute, and then the burly-looking guy with a beard says, "Of course it's appropriate—if Jenny here had done it, we'd have cut a half-hour off our wait time."

"Kevin," Jenny says, "You jerk." She smacks his arm.

"So that's a yes?" I ask.

"Yes," the men say, and the two women nod in agreement.

"Thanks," I say, and move on to the next table. I glance over at Jen and Marie, and they're laughing. The next table is three women, and although initially they say no, as I walk away they call me back to change their answer. The table after that are all guys, and they say yes before I've even asked the full question.

Jen looks embarrassed when I get back to the table, but Marie grins.

"Go Anna," Marie says. "What did they say?"

"Yeah, what did they say?" Jen asks.

"Well," I say, "everyone in this restaurant thinks its fine to flirt for a table."

"I knew it," Marie says.

"Brother," Jen says, and she stands up, ready to go. Marie and I follow her out. I wave at the two couples as we leave.

To my surprise, as we walk down the street away from the restaurant the cute manager comes running up behind us.

"Excuse me," he says, catching his breath as we turn around. "This is sort of awkward, but I, uh, was wondering if I could have your phone number."

"Well—" Marie says.

"No," he interrupts, "you." He looks right at Jen.

"Me?" Jen says.

I try so hard not to laugh when I see the shocked look on Jen's face.

"You're so beautiful," he says, and means it so sincerely that it's like Marie and I aren't even there. Jen blushes.

"I'm sorry," Jen says, "but I'm only seventeen, and you seem…"

"Oh," he says, surprised. "I thought you were much older."

"No," she says, "no I'm not."

He nods, embarrassed, and backs away. "Yeah," he says. "Okay, got it. Bye."

We watch him turn and go before we start laughing.

My technique improves over the course of the summer, and I gain confidence in myself. Most days are routine: technique class at ten, lunch with Jen and Marie at noon, *pointe* class at two, and either jazz, character, modern, or *pas de deux* at four. Charles Diamond looks in on my class once, but not enough to show any real interest in any of the summer students. He has a kind face, and he's shorter and older than Victor Caldwell, who was a colleague of his at BNY. I feel disappointed he doesn't teach our class.

The school combines the two upper levels for one class halfway through the summer, and it's the first time I've ever taken class with Jen. I think about how fun it will be when all three of us are in the same class at SBNY in the fall. I'm glad that Marie and I were both moved up at the end of the year.

Jen and Marie stand together at one of the portable *barres* and I find an empty place along the back wall. They've developed a competitive vibe, but it's friendly. I know I won't be able to work if I stand too close to my friends. I feel uncomfortable being competitive with them, and I'd rather keep my distance. Besides, if I stand near them I won't be able to focus in the same way, and I'll be tempted to whisper.

I do the splits and then put my right leg up on the *barre* to stretch. My body is in good shape after six weeks of intensive classes. Without school there's time to take three to four classes a day.

A tall man in tights and a t-shirt walks into the studio, our guest teacher from the company, Felipé Lopez. I like when he teaches, even though I feel like he's a little too cocky, and I'm not the only one. He's from Buenos Aires and came to San Francisco as a student when he was fifteen. Ten years later, he's a soloist in the company. His legs are beautifully shaped, and it's obvious he's trained more in classical ballet than Roizman by how formal and controlled he is just walking to the *barre*.

"He is so hot," the girl next to me whispers.

He claps his hands. "Let's begin," he says.

Felipé strolls around the room to inspect us as we begin the first combination. The atmosphere in his class is different than in New York, not any less serious or important, just slower and more relaxed. I stand with my heels touching and my toes pointing outwards in first position. I put my left hand on the *barre*. The *plié* combination begins as the pianist begins to play, and we move in unison. He stops to adjust Jen's arm and lift her chin up a fraction of an inch, and she glows with the attention. Marie stands up straighter at the same *barre*.

We move forward through the usual series of small footwork. My ankles, calves, knees, thighs, butt, stomach, abs, and back begin to feel warm. I focus on my biggest problem areas, the same corrections I get all the time: keeping my shoulders down and using my abdominal muscles to keep my back from swaying. Sweat and makeup starts dripping into my eyes by the time we start the *fondu* combination.

Forty-five minutes later, Felipé signals for us to clear the portable *barres* away. We come to the center of the room. People take a minute to stretch, put on their pointe shoes, or grab a drink of water. Jen, Marie, and I all have our pointe shoes on already, and after a year at SBNY, I can't imagine dancing in technique shoes, not even at the *barre*.

Felipé demonstrates the first center combination, pointing his feet to the front, back, side, and finishing with a turn. I mark the combination with my hands to memorize the sequence. Dancers slowly trickle back in and find their own space in the room.

"Let's go. First group," Felipé says. He is all professionalism, no smile, and I feel anxious to impress him, even though he seems stuck up. Jen and Marie stand right in front of the mirror. Most of the dancers from the higher class step forward. I stay in the back to observe, choosing to go with the second group. I like to have more time to watch and think about what I want to do. The music begins. I find myself watching Jen, who moves with grace and strength. In New York everyone is good, but here, it's glaringly obvious how talented Jen is. She's so far above almost everyone in the room that she's distracting.

The music ends, and Felipé crosses his arms and stands right in front of Marie. She's still holding the last pose, looking directly over her fingers to finish the line of her body. I feel a stab of jealousy that he might favor her, and do my best to push it away.

"An SBNY student," he says. I sense that he recognizes the signature style of her *pirouette*, the longer line in the preparation and finish. She nods and waits for him to correct her, but he doesn't, and so she drops her pose and straightens up to stare at him.

"I hate the SBNY style," he says.

Marie's mouth falls open. His bitterness surprises me too. Jen and I make eye contact across the room.

"You think that *pirouette* looks nice, but without both legs in *plié* at the beginning you have no solid foundation for your turn," he says. "Ridiculous. Show me a real *pirouette*."

And so Marie bends her back knee and does the *pirouette* again, flawlessly, the way dancers did it before Roizman influenced classical ballet. Felipé nods, "You see? Ha."

She nods and smiles at him, but I know that Marie, Jen, and I all think the other *pirouette* looked better, and suddenly I don't like him anymore, no matter how attractive he is. I'm sure that tomorrow Marie will be right back to doing it the SBNY way.

The class continues, but I feel my respect for Felipé Lopez fading and I'm not as interested in impressing him anymore. I find myself longing for my teachers in New York, especially Vivienne and Simon, and the comfort of SBNY. Dancing feels different when I've emotionally checked out. I keep watching the clock, waiting for it to be over.

Felipé gives easy, fun combinations to finish the class. Even though I like the steps, I feel frustrated with him for criticizing a style he doesn't agree with, rather than giving us new ideas to help us grow. The class is good though, because once I stop caring what he thinks, I dance with less inhibition. During the last combination, I waltz and leap with five other girls in a circle around the room. In the mirror my cheeks are bright red. It feels great to let my body fly at the end, when I'm completely warm.

Jen is stretching her calves on the tilted calf board when I walk over to her after I finish. A third group of girls form a circle in the middle of the room to repeat the exercise.

"Hey," Jen whispers to me. "I watched you today. You're pretty good."

We never comment on each other's dancing, so her comment takes me by surprise. It never occurred to me that she would watch me the way I watch her. I jump to the defensive. "Gee, thanks. You don't have to sound so surprised."

"No, that's not what I meant," Jen says, and I realize she's looking at me with new respect. "I just never saw you dance before."

"Oh," I say, "Thanks. That means a lot to me, coming from you. You're like the best dancer here."

She smiles. "Thanks," she says. "I'm so glad we're friends, Anna."

"Me too."

"Class dismissed," Felipé says, and the room breaks out in scattered applause. Jen and I walk to the back to pick up our bags. Everyone starts to file out of the room, and I feel a strong sense of dèja-vu, as just another class fades into the next. A powerful feeling of happiness washes over me.

We go to Union Square our last weekend, and after a few hours of shopping, we take a cable car to Fisherman's Wharf. It's crowded and humming with tourists. Jen is camera happy, and she walks in front of us, taking action shots.

"Cut it out," Marie says, charging ahead and ducking into the Ghirardelli chocolate store. We follow her. The store is filled with barrels of chocolate, and we wander through, tasting samples and picking out presents. I take my time, wanting the day to go on forever.

After I've paid, I walk outside to find my friends. They're sitting on a bench next to the pier. I wander over and sit down next to Marie.

"I do not know," Marie says, in the middle of the thought. "Sometimes I am not sure I want to get into a company. Everyone in BNY seems so miserable."

"Of course you do," Jen says. "Don't be silly. Once you're back in New York it'll come back to you. You left your family and came all the way from France to make it, I'm sure you still want to be a dancer."

"Are you serious, Marie?" I ask. "You don't think you want to be a dancer? What else would you do?" I feel shaken up by the thought.

"I am probably just in a phase," Marie says. "This summer has just been so nice. I do not feel like going back to all the competition and craziness. I want to keep having fun, eating whatever I want, and not worrying so much." She stands up and walks towards the railing. I've never seen her in such a reflective mood.

"I can't imagine quitting after everything we've already been through," Jen says. She seems worried about Marie, but I'm not. I can relate to Marie's feelings.

"I almost quit once," I say, "When I was thirteen. My mom and my ballet teacher talked me out of it. I thought I wanted to focus on horseback riding, which was stupid, because we couldn't afford it anyway. I don't think my parents realized how expensive the pointe shoes would get. I can't imagine quitting now."

"I'd never quit now," Jen says.

"I am thinking about joining the circus," Marie says, turning away from us to lean over the railing and looking in the water.

We're quiet for a moment, just thinking. After awhile, Marie turns back around and faces us. She crosses her arms.

"Marie," I say, "your sweater." I point. The sleeves of her nice black cardigan are covered in goop.

She looks at her elbows and shrieks.

"I think that stuff keeps the birds away," Jen says.

"Gross!" Marie says. "My good sweater…"

"Oh no," I say. "I'm sorry."

"Ugh," Marie says. "Let's go."

We catch the bus home. Marie makes crepes for dinner, and after we eat, we turn the radio on full blast and start to pack.

Eventually I crawl into bed, but it takes me a long time to fall asleep. I'm excited to see Vivienne, Simon, and Tyler again, and be back in New York, but I feel sad that the summer is almost over. I'm in love with Marie's wild streak, Jen's sincerity, and the way I feel when we're together. We had so many good times this summer that I'm sure our friendship will last a lifetime. I don't want anything to change.

Chapter 7

We're back in New York by the end of August. Jen and I are roommates, and it makes me grateful last year is over. Without Hilary, I feel happy on a daily basis. Marie and I are in the upper class of the advanced division now, which seems like an adjustment for Jen, used to being ahead of us, and for me, used to being behind. It's nice to see Tyler and all the other guys again, but Nicole and Hilary I could do without.

On the first day, Simon is indicating a small jump combination when the door opens and the director of National Ballet Theatre, Bruce Pollock, walks into the studio. He's a tall bald man with spectacles. I'm surprised to see him here. NBT is the other major company in New York besides SBNY, and the leading classical ballet troupe in the United States.

Simon stops in the middle of his demonstration to walk over and shake Bruce Pollock's hand. They whisper while we stand around and wait. I feel nervous and excited.

"What's he doing here?" I ask Marie. We huddle together in the back of the studio.

She rises up and down on pointe, looking nervous too. "No idea," she whispers back.

The discussion at the front of the room drags on. I study myself in the mirror. I feel like it's a skinny day. NBT dancers aren't as tall as at BNY, so I feel like maybe I should think more about their company. I try to read what Simon and Bruce Pollock are saying with no luck, but they seem to be looking at Jen.

Simon gestures to us, indicating the *petit allegro* one more time. "Ready," he says. Bruce Pollock takes a seat at the front of the room.

The rest of the class feels like an audition. Nicole and Hilary push their way to the front, repeating every combination several times, and I can't help feeling irritated by them. Jen also goes in front, but she has the most seniority in our class so it feels appropriate. I'm anxious and uncomfortable, so I stick behind Marie in the second group. Marie is typically more forward than I am, and she's sometimes competitive with Jen, but today she hangs back. I don't feel like she's intimidated the way I am. It almost seems like Marie doesn't care. By the end we're all dripping with sweat.

We finish the *grand révérance* at the end and everyone claps. Bruce Pollock stands and walks over to whisper to Simon. He's so comfortable watching and evaluating us that it's easy to respect him, even though he's disrupted our day. It feels important to have him here.

"Will Jen please stay after for a moment," Simon announces.

I feel my stomach drop. There's a half-second of hesitation, and then we all go about our business as if nothing out of the ordinary has happened. Jen walks slowly to the front of the room, and she seems completely calm, even though I'm sure she must be coming out of her own skin. I pick up my bag and walk out in the hallway to sit and take off my pointe shoes.

I'm sure NBT must have an opening, or Bruce Pollock wouldn't be here. I can't believe I feel so emotional over something I didn't even know I wanted. Of course Jen is the best in the class. Of course she is. But what's wrong with me?

Jen walks out of the studio after a few minutes, smiling. She seems so happy, and she leans over and whispers to me, "He invited me to take class with NBT tomorrow." I stare at her as she squeezes my hand, giddy with excitement.

"Congratulations!" I say. I feel happy for her but part of me is jealous too.

"I can't believe it," she says. "This felt like any other day. I've got to call my parents." She drops my hand and walks down the hall.

I watch her go, feeling amazed at how quickly something like this can happen. It seems like we were just teenagers in San Francisco, and almost overnight, Jen's going to be a professional ballerina. I always knew she would be. I'm so proud to be her friend.

The next morning, Jen wakes up at the same time I do for the first time ever. She leaves to go downtown to the NBT studios before I leave for school.

"*Merde*," I tell her, which we say for good luck. She smiles but she looks pale, the most nervous I've ever seen her.

I think about Jen all day, as I sit through Algebra and French, as I take morning technique class, at lunch, and during American History. By pointe class I'm dying to know what happened. If Jen gets into NBT, she'll get to have that moment we've all been dreaming of, where she tells her family and her local ballet school that she made it. I'd give anything in the world to call my parents and tell them I'd been offered a job.

Jen is sitting in our windowsill, looking out at the plaza when I walk into our room after pointe class. Her profile is beautiful, and I can feel the determination coming out of her. She turns her head.

"Well?" I ask.

"They offered me an apprenticeship," she says.

"Oh my God," I say as I run over to hug her.

"Everyone at home is going to freak out," Jen says. "I'll get to dance *La Bayadère* and *Giselle* and *Romeo and Juliet*. I'd never dance that stuff at BNY."

I sit down in the windowsill across from her. "You're definitely taking it?" If she does, she'll shut the door to BNY. Trying to go from NBT to BNY is like trying to go from the Mets to the Yankees.

"Yeah," she says. She nods and bites her lip. I feel the weight of her dilemma.

"What about BNY?"

"Madame Sivenko told me to take the job."

"Oh." I can only imagine how much that must have hurt to hear. Jen is probably the best dancer in the school right now, but she's also the only one left from last year's Advanced class. Everyone else quit or got a job already.

"Victor Caldwell says I have a weight problem," she says, and I feel horrible for her.

"But you're a stick." She hardly eats; only cereal and vegetables.

"I know what you're thinking," she says.

"I was thinking how hard you've worked and how an accomplishment this is." I look out the window, but she stares at me until I have to meet her gaze.

"I'll never be skinny enough for them," she says. Her voice seems flat.

"NBT is a great company."

"Oh, shut up, Anna," she says. "I'm a failure."

"A failure?" I'm taken aback and my hands start to shake. She's been handed this incredible opportunity and all she can thing about is how she didn't get in to Ballet New York.

"I've been planning to join BNY since I was a little girl," she says. "They asked me to do something, I did it. The teachers told me to lose weight all the time. I've been anorexic, bulimic, taken laxatives—you name it."

I can't believe she says it out loud. I knew she was doing it, but we never discussed it. Don't ask, and don't tell.

"You know what else?" she says. "I've been having trouble…Anna, sometimes I cut myself."

"Jen…" I don't want to know.

"Look." She stands up, unbuttons her jeans, and pulls them down. I can't believe I never noticed it through her tights, but now that I think about it, she wears a skirt in ballet class whenever she can get away with it.

Her upper thighs are covered with scars. There are fresh scabs too, razor marks.

I feel a shooting pain across my stomach. "Oh God."

"It makes me feel better and reminds me that I'm a human," she says. "The blood proves I'm not dead. I feel dead sometimes. I can't control my genes. How am I supposed to stop puberty?"

"You just got into one of the top ballet companies in the world," I say, feeling like I'm going to cry. "You should be celebrating."

"But it doesn't mean anything," she says, and I feel like she believes it. She puts her jeans back on and sits down on her bed.

"Look Jen, maybe you should talk to someone about this."

"I'm talking to you," she says. "Who else would I talk to? People outside don't understand."

I nod. She's right. Anyone who hasn't been in the dance world wouldn't understand.

Chapter 8

Jen's quick departure leaves a void in the advanced class. I miss having her to look up to, but her absence pushes me to grow. I didn't mind standing in the back when Jen was in the front, but now that she's gone, I don't want Hilary and Nicole to be the stars of the class. So I start to go in front. And I start to believe I belong there.

As the weeks roll by, I feel like my body and the way I dance changes. I notice I don't breeze through combinations anymore. Instead, I start thinking about every detail of my movements, and my dancing finally starts to become a craft. I envision how I want a step to look, and more and more, I can make that vision into reality. For years, I felt like I was struggling to translate the ideal into the physical, and all of a sudden, after almost fifteen years of training, I feel like I know how to apply it. I can tell I think and move with a new level of awareness.

Victor Caldwell teaches our class in November. It's the first time he's seen any of us dance, and I feel like we've never been so nervous or so cutthroat. It seems like he brings out our best and our worst.

"Gee, everyone seems so tense," Hilary announces breezily as I walk in the door. She has on a new low-cut velvet leotard, and she keeps checking everyone out. "I heard Victor is already thinking about who he wants to give apprenticeships to next spring, after workshop…Oh my gosh, Faye, do you think you should be wearing those legwarmers? I'd wear mine, but I don't want him to think I'm hiding cellulite or anything. Nicole, is my stomach sticking out today? God I feel bloated." She turns sideways to look at her reflection and pooches her stomach out.

Faye, always quiet, peels off her legwarmers.

"I'm the one who looks horrible," Nicole says. "Look how fat I am. And my skin—call me the acne monster." She walks up to the mirror and examines her pores. Hilary makes a nasty face behind Nicole's back.

"Will they ever shut up?" Marie whispers to me as we tie the ribbons on our pointe shoes. I smile and keep my head down.

"Hey Anna," Hilary calls across the room. "Yo! Linado."

I look up. "What?"

"Don't stand by me today," she says. "I don't want you highlighting what a big fat cow I am."

I feel a rush of irritation. "Okay," I say.

Vivienne follows Victor Caldwell into the room looking anxious, and I can feel what a big day this is for her too. She barely comes up to his chest. His teaching outfit is jeans, a t-shirt, and sneakers. On first impression he doesn't seem like a nice man, and actually, he seems like the kind of person who thinks he knows everything. He walks over and leans on the piano, scanning the room for several minutes before he claps his hands to begin. Vivienne sits down in front to observe. I feel her nitpicking each of us with her eyes.

The first half of the class doesn't go well. At the *barre* Victor focuses only on Nicole, spending a full five minutes analyzing her *tendu*. It's all I can do not to scream, and looking around the room, I see every other girl going crazy in her own head. Only Nicole looks happy. The rest of us already seem devastated.

His class is simple, and seems designed only to observe us, not necessarily to teach us anything. I want to be what he's looking for, whatever that is, but I get no indication of what he wants. And incredibly, wanting to be something is enough.

"You," Victor says, pointing at me in the back line as I finish a jump combination. "Come here." His voice is commanding.

I walk forward to the center of the room, surprised he's been watching me even though it's what I was desperately hoping for. His eyes seem to look everywhere at once throughout the class, and I can't read his expression at all.

"Class, watch," he says.

The others form a half circle, some watching my image in the mirror and some watching me directly. I step into fifth position to repeat the combination, feeling Vivienne's eyes on me. The pianist plays an introduction; *Five, six, seven, eight…* I launch myself into the air. *Sissone, assemblé. Sissone, assemblé.* I think the steps in my head at the same time that I dance them. *Sous-sous, entrechat six. Sous-sous, entrechat six.*

"Good," Victor says. The class claps politely for me. "Notice how she emphasizes the musical retards. Roizman ballets are visual representations of the music, so you must let sound create the impetus in your body. You should be thinking ahead and anticipating what's next, but you cannot dance off the music. It takes confidence and trust to believe that your body will do exactly the right thing in the right moment, but you must learn to trust yourself. There's magic to being musical, because it can't exist without an innate willingness to be in the moment, and doing all the *pliés* in the world can't give that to you. You're the only one who can give it to yourself."

We nod, trying to understand.

"I get it," Hilary says. Victor Caldwell pretends not to hear her.

"I need to *see* the music when you do the combination," he says. "Don't forget to take a deeper *plié* before the *entrechat six*." He nods at me. "She's the only one clearly giving me all six beats."

I'm not sure what I did, but I feel elated.

After class is over, I collapse on the floor in the hallway. My body aches, I'm sore in muscles I didn't know I had, and I tingle all over, but I feel happy.

I sit up to untie my pointe shoes. One of the younger students walks over to me. Her face is familiar because she looks in on the advanced class whenever our door is open. I've seen her mom in the hallway a lot, a serious ballet mom. "You're my favorite dancer in the school," she says. Her hair is pulled back tight.

"Wow. Thanks." She reminds me of my own thirteen-year old reflection. I see my own obsession in her eyes.

"I'd give anything to have your feet," she says.

"Let me see yours."

She blushes but points her foot for me. Her arch is high in her instep, already a beautiful bow shaped arc.

"I'll trade you."

"Okay!"

I smile at her.

"How do you always look so happy when you dance?" she asks.

"I do?" I'm stunned.

She nods, and all I can do is stare at her, surprised at how little I know myself.

"Hey, Linado." Tyler passes me on his way to the studio. He leans over and squeezes my shoulder, which snaps me out of a daze. I look up at him. Before he walks off he winks at me, and my heart leaps inside my chest. I notice that his back is solid muscle as he walks into the studio, and he's grown several inches over the summer. He's turning into a man.

I walk down the hall towards the water fountain. Before I round the corner, I bend down to pull up my leg warmers. Nicole's voice floats around the corner. "I can't believe Victor had Anna demonstrate."

"She sucks," Hilary says.

"Now Hilary, let's be nice," Nicole says.

"That bitch needs to get over herself," Hilary says. "I wouldn't be smiling if I were that short. I'd be filling out my college applications."

I hesitate, filling up with familiar anger, and walk around the corner. "Hey guys."

They hardly blink. "Hi Anna," Nicole says. She smiles.

"Were you talking about me?"

Hilary smiles. "Why would we be talking about you?" she asks innocently.

Nicole averts her eyes. They walk right past me without another word.

As soon as they're gone I kick my foot into the wall so hard I scream. The tears come and they don't stop, not for the rest of the day, the week even.

I'm hurt by what they said, even though I can't stand them. I want people to like me. I need approval and I know it. It feels like a physical wound when I've displeased anyone, especially if it was unintentional. I think that's a big part of why I dance. The appreciation of beauty, the thrill of escapism, and the applause and appreciation of an audience are major reasons why I wanted to be a dancer. That kind of love creates the world my parents were never able to give me. If hatred and bitterness is the reality of the dance world, the original reason I fell in love with ballet seems to have gone up in smoke.

SBNY agrees to let Jen remain in the dorm through the rest of the school year even though she's already started her apprenticeship with NBT. I'm glad I don't have to deal with a new roommate, even though I feel left behind whenever Jen talks about her new experiences as a member of a real company.

We spend many evenings in our room, playing music and taking our personal quiet time. We never discuss the eating disorders or the cutting anymore, not since the day she got in to NBT. Most nights, she sews shoes on the floor and I sit at my desk, lost in French exercises or English papers, complicit in our silence.

After we come back from the Thanksgiving holiday, Jen talks me into hanging Christmas lights in our room. The first year we lived together I was against it, but by now I don't care as much. I don't live with my parents anymore, and I like the commercial aspect of Christmas. Besides, I feel like things have been good. Victor Caldwell noticed me, Vivienne's been correcting me all the time, Hilary and Nicole act like I'm real competition, and the school in New Jersey hired me for the *Nutcracker* this year. I'm beginning to feel like my goal to join BNY is within reach, if only I would grow another two inches. Ballet school doesn't feel overwhelming anymore. I've started to think I'm almost ready to turn professional.

The phone rings and Jen answers it. I'm standing on the desk, thumb-tacking a row of lights across our ceiling and not paying attention.

"It's for you," Jen says. "A guy."

I have no idea who it could be. The only people who call me are my parents and Rachel. "That's weird." I jump off the desk and walk over to pick up the phone. "Hello?"

"Anna?"

"Yeah?"

"It's Tyler."

"Tyler?" My mouth goes dry. He's never called me before. Last year he just always used to drop in, but we never seem to hang out anymore. I feel like he's grown away from me since last year.

"Yeah," he says.

"What's up?" I ask.

He pauses. "I'm down in the lobby," he says. "I forgot my ID card, and there's a new security guy who won't let me in."

"Oh," I say. "Well, I'll come down and get you. It's almost curfew."

"Thanks," he says, and hangs up.

"That was Tyler," I say, and Jen gives me a funny look.

"He likes you," she says.

I feel my heart speed up. "No he doesn't," I say. "We're just friends. He forgot his ID. I have to go save him from security."

"Okay," Jen says. She smirks before she goes back to reading her upcoming tour schedule. I ignore her to check myself in the mirror, wondering if I look okay in jeans, a cream sweater, and flip-flops. I hate to admit it, but I'm excited at the prospect of seeing Tyler while I'm wearing normal clothes, with my hair down, after ballet hours.

I take the elevator downstairs. The door opens and there he is, sitting all spread out on a bench in the lobby. He's wearing a dress shirt and jeans, and his eyes are closed. I push through the turnstile, walk over, and sit down next to him. He's wearing cologne—something musky that seems too grown up for him.

"Hey sleepy," I say, nudging him. "Curfew in five."

"Oh hi," he says with his eyes closed.

"Where have you been?" I ask, and he's quiet long enough to make me feel intimidated, and it bothers me. When did things get awkward between us?

"I had a date," he says.

I'm shocked, and I pause for a moment before I respond. "With who?"

"Bergitte Pedersen," he says.

I don't believe it. "The gorgeous new Danish girl in the corps of BNY?"

"Yep," he says, running a hand through his hair.

"You're such a liar," I say.

"No lie," he says. "She's been flirting with me at company parties."

"Since when do you go to company parties?" I ask.

"I have friends in high places," he says, standing up. "Come on." He takes my hand and pulls me up next to him, so close that our faces almost touch. I step back.

"Well, good for you," I say. I walk over to the security guard and show him my ID. He nods and lets Tyler through the gate while I go through the turnstile. Tyler follows me into the elevator.

"Do you like her?" I ask him while we ride up, and I can feel my frustration growing. He won't make eye contact, he keeps his eyes fixed on the numbers, and I can't read him at all. The elevator door dings and opens on his floor.

"Do you like her?" I ask again.

He shrugs. "I like someone else more," he says. He glances over his shoulder as he walks out of the elevator, but the doors close before I can figure out how to respond.

Marie and I walk across the plaza late one Thursday night in December on the way home from a trip to Tower Records. White flakes stick to our hair and eyelashes, the first real snow of the year. The smoking crowd, always led by Charlie and Nicole, is out in front of the door to the building. Vivienne yells at them whenever she walks by and sees them smoking, not that it does any good.

A lot of the company members and students smoke cigarettes. It looks cool, it's a bonding exercise and a ritual, and most importantly, it suppresses appetite. The smokers have a tougher time breathing when they dance, but they get by. Our bodies may be our instruments, but even though I don't smoke because I hate the smell, I think of my body in the moment, not in terms of longevity. I think we want instant gratification and don't care about later. Later it won't matter, because the best part of our lives will already be over. What's a little lung cancer down the road? Thinking ahead--beyond a dance career--is too unfathomable.

"Since when are Tyler and Jamal part of that crowd?" Marie asks. Jesse and Tyler are leaning against the railing next to each other, and there's a cigarette curling gray plumes of smoke up into the air from between Tyler's fingers. Hilary, Nicole, Jamal, and Charlie are huddled in a small half-circle a few feet away, also smoking.

"I don't know." I've never seen Tyler smoking before.

We reach them and Marie goes over to talk to Jamal. I see the way Jamal smiles when he sees her, and wonder if she notices too. I walk up next to Tyler. He's in the middle of telling Jesse a story. "...he eloped with this hot physical therapist who worked with all the dancers," Tyler says. "All the girls in the company were heartbroken."

"William Mason," Jesse says, catching my eye. "The legend of Ballet New York. Tyler's educating me."

"Yeah, William Mason was a god." I've read William Mason's autobiography and the two other books written about him.

"Anna's idol is Stacy Hannah," Tyler says.

"She was amazing!" I say. "The original *Fire* girl. Short, fast, all personality. Stacy Hannah and William Mason had one of the best partnerships ever." I want to be Stacy Hannah.

"What a bunhead," Jesse says, but his smile is warm and friendly. "You're worse than all the girls back home in Houston."

"William Mason was the original lead in *Fire*," Tyler says. He takes a long drag.

"He shattered the image that all male ballet dancers are gay," I say.

"Of course they're not all gay," Jesse says. "Look at me."

"Anna has more important things to do," Tyler says rudely.

"Excuse me?" I say, embarrassed. "Since when do you run my life?"

They laugh, but I don't understand why Tyler's acting so standoffish towards me. He's been more and more distant since this year started, and the more I try to ignore it, the weirder things get between us. We never even go to the ballet or dance together in *pas de deux* class anymore.

Tyler looks across the plaza at theater-goers walking through the snow. I pick up bits of the other conversations: Charlie telling Nicole and Hilary about a drag queen hitting on him at a club last weekend; Jamal trying to teach Marie the words to Tupac's *Me Against the World* and laughing at her French accent. Tyler shuffles his feet and takes another drag.

"Do you know William Mason's story?" I ask, trying to recover.

Jesse and Tyler look at me and say nothing.

"Well then, I'll tell you," I say. "He was born on a horse farm in Montana. His dad wanted him to be a rancher, but whenever he ran errands in town he saw the girls going to ballet lessons. One day he followed a girl he had a crush on and the teacher got him to take the class. So of course he fell in love with the girl and got completely hooked on dance."

"Sounds familiar," Jesse says. He hops up on the ledge and lets his legs swing back and forth. Tyler leans against the ledge next to him. I admire them. Jesse, handsome but untouchable, and Tyler, warm and cute— they make a good-looking pair.

"His father didn't find out for two years that he was taking ballet," I continue. "Then one day, he happened to be in town and saw William coming out of dance class with his ballet shoes in hand. He beat him up bad. William had one more year left of high school left, but he ran away from home. His girlfriend was obsessed with Ballet New York, so he had it in his head that was the place he'd go. So he hitchhiked all the way New York, slept in Central Park, bagged groceries, and eventually

SBNY took him. A few months later, Roizman stopped by the school, saw him flying around the room, and invited him to join the company."

"And then," Tyler says, "He had a twenty-five year career of standing ovations, honors, awards, TV, over thirty Roizman ballets choreographed for him, including *Fire*, and covers of *Dance*, *Time*, *Newsweek*, *Vanity Fair*, the works."

"Plus he slept with practically every girl in the company," I say.

"And now he's the director of Los Angeles Ballet Theatre," Jesse says.

"One of the top companies in the country," Tyler says.

"But he's not Victor Caldwell," I say.

"William Mason is better than Victor Caldwell," Tyler says. "Victor Caldwell was nowhere near as exciting a dancer, and he's stupid enough to try to run Roizman's company after Roizman died. William Mason and Stacy Hannah were invited to dance at the White House for three different presidents."

We're quiet for a moment, picturing it. Jesse stands up and stretches his arms over his head. He yawns before crossing his arms and leaning back against the ledge next to Tyler. It's cold outside, but the plaza is romantic after dark when it's bathed in the light from the Metropolitan Opera House and New York State Theater. I can only imagine what it must have been like for Stacy

Hannah and William Mason the night of the original premiere of *Fire*.

The moment evaporates when Hilary walks over to Jesse and puts her arms around his shoulders. "Hi honey," she whispers, making sweet with him, but Jesse's not having it. Tyler and I exchange a glance.

Jesse uncrosses his arms and takes a step towards me. "I've been thinking I should try dancing with you in *pas* class," he says to me.

"What are you talking about?" I ask, taken completely by surprise, but before I even finish Jesse picks me up by the waist and twirls me around.

"Hey. Put me down," I say. I can feel Tyler and Hilary watching and it makes me uncomfortable.

"But you're so light," Jesse says. He holds me over his head, looking up at me. The more I struggle the more it amuses him, and finally he lowers me to the ground, slowly, letting my body slide against his.

"What the heck, Jesse," Tyler says. "Quit bothering her."

"I'm not bothering her," Jesse says, letting go of my waist and taking my hand. "We're having a conversation." He doesn't take his eyes off me. I haven't let myself really think about any guy in so long that the sudden attention from Jesse makes my heart pound.

I glance at Marie, Jamal, Nicole, and Charlie, and they're staring at me. Hilary is glaring at me too. I look at Tyler, most concerned about his reaction, but he's looking at the ground.

"I'm going in," Tyler announces. He grinds his cigarette out with his shoe and walks off towards the building.

"Hey! Tyler!" I pull away from Jesse, worried that I've made Tyler mad.

But Tyler doesn't look back. He's already disappeared inside by the time I've started after him, and I stop, unsure what I should do.

"Are you going in?" Marie asks me, breaking away from the other group.

"It's early, baby," Jamal says, grabbing her hand. A flicker of indecision crosses her face.

I look past him and see that Charlie and Nicole are hugging now to keep warm, and Hilary is just standing there, looking mad.

I make eye contact with Jesse, who seems hurt.

Hilary walks over and puts her hand on Jesse's shoulder, looking up at him. He glances down at her for a second. He looks back after Tyler and at me. She sees it, and it's obvious she doesn't like it.

Jesse waits for a minute and when I don't say anything he turns to her and says, "Hey, I was just playing around."

"Let's go," I say, grabbing Marie's arm, pulling her away from Jamal. We walk into the building. She doesn't say a word about the scene on the plaza, but I can't get it out of my head for hours. I lie in bed and relive them listening to me tell the story about William Mason, Jesse picking me up, putting his arms around me,

Tyler watching and not watching and storming away. I play it over and over in my head, but I still don't know what it means.

Chapter 9

Jesse's behavior seems more erratic and hard to understand. He flirts increasingly with me when we see each other in the dorms, at school, in the cafeteria, and especially in front of Tyler. He acts like we have an inside joke. Even though I'm flattered by the attention, Jesse's motives feel insincere, whatever they are. And he starts to act downright nasty towards Tyler, which bothers me more than it seems to bother Tyler. But the harder I try not to appear allied with Jesse, the more Tyler pulls away from me.

Tyler stops speaking to me. I'm not sure what I've done wrong, but he acts as if I don't exist. And the more Tyler ignores me, the more I feel like I need to talk to him. It becomes difficult for me to think about ballet or school. When I'm not thinking about him, I'm trying to figure out if Jesse actually likes me. My mind can't focus on day-to-day things. I get to be so on edge I irritate myself. Vivienne and Madame Sivenko correct me and I barely hear them. Ballet feels like a means to an end, just a way to see what will happen next. I forget myself.

Simon's class becomes my refuge. His constant silence finally makes sense to me, because of how much he leaves me to myself. It comes to me on my own terms why everyone thinks Simon is a genius, how it applies to me, not just how I'm expected to believe in it. I feel safe exposing my heart in a room of silence. The freedom from judgment takes away the risk of dancing poorly. I stop focusing on conventions, tradition, and accepted form in his class, because I'm so hung up on boys I don't care about those things right now. All Simon expects is for us to focus on ourselves, and the more I do it the better I dance. My head somehow clears, and I feel pure. It seems to me that the magic of performance is as much in the attention of a captive audience as in the act of dancing itself.

Jen, who I hardly see now that she's in NBT, is more focused on her new company friends and her career, and Marie is consumed with her feelings for Jamal, who seems so focused on her he hardly talks to anyone else anymore. When I do talk to Jen or Marie, I find I say the same thing over and over: "Why does Tyler hate me now? What happened?" and they have no answers and can offer me no help.

Marie, Jamal, and I go to BNY's season opening gala together. Jamal is growing on me, and it's not just that I'm just more patient with him because I don't want to lose Marie as a friend. He's considerate of Marie in a way I never would have expected.

The company dances one of my favorite classic Roizman ballets, *America*. The music is Sousa and it involves the whole company, a real spectacle ballet. Diana Rampling and Richard Jackson dance the *pas de deux*, and they're terrific, bold and full of energy and excitement.

"The Paris Opera dancers can't move that fast," I say, teasing Marie as we walk past the fountain on our way home.

"Ha," she says. "But the theater is no Opéra Garnier."

"Marie, girl, you know you loved it," Jamal says. "Those bitches rocked."

We laugh and then grow silent, thinking about just how good it was.

"I did love it," Marie says, growing serious. "I have to get in to the company, I just have to."

"We all want to get in," I say.

"No, Anna," she snaps. "I *have* to get in. This is not fun and games. My parents did not send me all the way from France to not get in."

Jamal stares at the ground while I swallow and wonder how to respond. I think Marie has a good chance, but none of us know for sure. There just aren't any guarantees.

Up ahead I see Tyler walking into the building with Charlie and Hilary. "Why does he hang out with them?" I ask, hurt.

"I don't know," Marie says. "But you need to get over it."

"I know!" But I can't seem to.

Marie and Jamal say good night to me when we get upstairs, and he follows her to her room. I can hear Jamal humming the music to *America* as he disappears. It makes me smile.

I open my door and let out a sigh. Jen is performing with NBT, and my room is lonely and dull after the excitement of the ballet. I sit on my bed in my dress, wishing I could talk to Tyler about the show. Last year we used to dissect every performance together. It takes me twenty minutes to work up the nerve to walk downstairs to his room, which depresses me because I used to stop by all the time.

The light is on in his room and I hear laughter behind the door. I'm not sure if I should knock so I just stand there.

It startles me when Tyler's door opens a crack and he sticks his head out. "I thought I heard something," he says. He's still dressed up from the gala and his tie is hanging loose around his neck. His hair is rumpled.

"Hi."

"What are you doing here?' he asks. His eyes are red and he won't look at me.

"I came to visit you."

He runs a hand through his hair, processing.

"Who's there?" Charlie says from behind Tyler's door.

"Anna," Tyler says.

"Anna!" Charlie says happily.

"Hey Charlie." I brush past Tyler and walk into his room. Charlie is sitting on the corner of the bed. I stop when I see Hilary, her red hair spilled out on the pillow, is lying down next to him.

"Oh hi," Hilary says.

"Hey." I've never seen either of them in Tyler's room before. The room is a mess. There are potato chips all over the floor and the carpet hasn't been vacuumed in weeks. I look over at the small fridge, and there's a bottle of Smirnoff vodka on top, right in plain view. The staff never comes in anyway.

Tyler follows me into the room, passing me to open the window, and my nose fills with the smell of pot. It makes me gag. Charlie is holding a joint.

"Did the little princess come to smoke?" Hilary asks. She props herself up on her elbow and looks me over.

"No thanks." I lean against the dresser, wishing I had never come down the stairs.

Tyler sits down at his desk chair, shooting me a dirty look. Charlie passes the joint to Hilary. She takes a drag and then passes it to Tyler, who keeps his eyes on me as he takes it. He waits for a long time before he brings it to his lips, watching me carefully. The low hum of the stereo is the only sound in the room.

It's horrible to watch the most talented guy I've ever known do this, if only because it kills me to see him take for granted all the things I'll never have. His future is so secure. I can't believe I used to think we had so much in common.

"Anna, don't look upset," Charlie says.

"She's such a baby," Hilary says with disgust.

They laugh and laugh, and very quietly, I back up and slip out the door, trying desperately to hold it together until I can get back to my room. Once there, I curl up in a tiny ball on my bed. I lie there wondering why I feel so angry and distanced from everyone I know. I feel like no one gets me.

The week of finals before the *Nutcracker* in New Jersey, I'm preoccupied with school. It's actually a relief to have something concrete to focus on, like math. My thinking about Tyler is circular; it gets me nowhere. I spend every night at my desk, poring over my books, determined to get good grades on my exams. Jen is gone on tour with NBT to California, so I have the room to myself.

By ten o'clock the night before my last final I can't sit still. I grab some change and head for the elevators to hit up the vending machines in the lobby. When the elevator opens, I walk right into Jesse before he even has a chance to get off.

"Oops," I say, blushing. I've been avoiding him lately.

"What's the rush?" he asks, standing in the way so the doors don't close. He's wearing khakis and a black polo shirt and looks great.

"No rush. I just need a chocolate fix."

"That sounds good," he says, and steps back into the elevator with me. The doors close.

"Where are you coming from?" I ask.

"Dinner with my grandparents," he says. It's the first time I've ever heard anything about his family.

"Do they live here?"

"No," he says, "they're visiting from Michigan."

"I'm, uh, I didn't know."

"It's okay," he says. "They raised me. They're kinda like my parents." We stand across from each other, leaning against opposite sides of the elevator.

"What happened to your real parents?"

"They died when I was little," he says.

"Oh."

"They were in a car accident," he explains.

"I'm so sorry." I can't believe I've known him for two years but didn't know about it.

We cross the lobby towards the room where the vending machines are tucked away. I glance at his profile. He suddenly seems like someone I don't know at all.

"Did your grandparents want you to be a dancer?" I ask.

"My parents were both dancers with BNY," he tells me, and I'm even more shocked I didn't know this either. The vending machine room is small and I have to stand close to him. He smells good, like soap. I watch him drop quarters into the machine and press the button for Twix.

"It seemed natural for me to apply here, but the truth is, I kind of want to do something totally different," he says, glancing at me. "I like school." He retrieves his candy from the bottom slot.

I step in front of him to put my change in the machine and get my Reese's peanut butter cups, fully conscious of the fact that he's standing right behind me. His presence makes me feel self-conscious, and my stomach flutters when I turn around to face him.

He leans forward and kisses me on the lips, running a hand through my hair. For a moment he just presses his mouth against mine, and then he steps closer, kissing me harder. His hands move from my hair to cup my face.

I'm the one who pulls away. "Why did you do that?" I ask, shocked and pleased.

He shrugs. "Why not Anna?"

I try to stop myself from smiling but I can't help it. He smiles too. Then he pulls me in his arms and kisses me again, harder. It's good, and frightening because I'm not used to feeling out of control. I push him away.

"We should go back upstairs," I say finally, a little out of breath.

"Why?" he asks. "Are you afraid of me?" I am.

"You're trouble." I finally answer.

"No I'm not," he says, and for a moment I believe him.

We get back in the elevator. He reaches for me again but I move away. "That's enough."

"Why?" he asks, and he looks hurt. I can't explain why he makes me so nervous, and I'm relieved when the elevator doors open. I'm halfway down the hall towards my suite before he grabs my wrist. I glance around. I don't want people to see us.

"Don't leave," he says. "Come over to my room. We can just talk. I want to spend time with you, Anna."

"I can't." I pull my hand away. He gives me the same hurt look, but I can't let this go any farther. I back away down the hall, turning away from him when I reach the corner towards my suite. When I get in my room I shut the door and lean against it, slowly sliding down to a sitting position. I sigh. Thank goodness Jen's gone and I can be alone. There's something about Jesse I don't trust, and the thought of us together doesn't feel right even though I'm attracted to him. The way he kissed me wasn't how I imagined kissing would feel. It felt more like a performance than like love. I bring my hands to my cheeks and feel how warm they are. Jesse was my first kiss.

Jesse keeps his distance during the last week before winter break, even when we all go to New Jersey for *Nutcracker*. Marie and I share a hotel room and I eat all my meals with her and Jamal. I dance Doll, Snow, and Marzipan, and it's the first time I've performed in a year and a half, since Rock Island. Performing makes me so happy. It makes me feel complete and takes everything I have.

I spend an hour before the shows pulling my wet hair into a perfect tight bun, carefully applying base, eyeshadow, eyeliner, false eyelashes, blush, and red lipstick. I love the red, white, and blue patchwork satin Doll tutu, the silver and white Snow tutu and silver crown, and the yellow tutu with pink flowers I wear for Marzipan. Everyone looks beautiful, dressed up and in full makeup, at their best. The lights add a larger-than-life feeling to everything that happens onstage, and standing in the wings, I'm overwhelmed by how proud I am to be part of something that brings beauty and happiness into people's lives. I feel important standing on pointe on the stage before the curtain goes up on Act II, just watching everyone prepare to shine. My life means something.

It's easy to avoid both Tyler and Jesse, especially because from what I hear Tyler spends the whole week getting drunk and high in the hotel with Charlie and Hilary. I don't understand how Tyler manages to perform, but he does—they all do. Charlie and Hilary look exhausted, but Tyler's dancing is more brilliant than ever.

Hilary and Nicole are in a fight, and Nicole and Jesse are together all the time, much to Hilary's obvious irritation. I try not to wonder what's going on between them. If Jesse's trying to make me feel bad, it's not going to work. I know better than to think he meant it when he kissed me. Jesse doesn't seem sincerely interested in Nicole, but then again, he didn't seem sincerely interested in me either. But she seems caught up in him.

It's a relief to go home for winter break, and Mom picks me up from the airport. Sammy climbs in my lap and licks my hand. I'm so happy to see him. I think I miss my dog more than anything else.

"We're considering selling the house," she says. Her face looks drawn and tired, and she forgets to put on her blinker and do a head check before switching lanes. The guy she cuts off honks at us.

"I hoped we would be able to keep it until he retires," she says. "But we can barely afford the house as it is, and who knows what your situation will be next year."

They made so many sacrifices so I could go to SBNY.

"You won't have to worry about paying for college," I say. "I'll have a full time job next year dancing."

"Maybe, maybe not," she says. "Anna, we want you to go to college, whether it's next year or a few years from now." They've obviously discussed it with each other at length, but this is the first time I've heard of it.

"I don't think you get it. Ballet is a *career*. I'm not going to college." I look out the window at the cozy houses and tree-lined streets and can't imagine ever going back to this kind of life.

"Yes, Anna," she says. "I know. I'm just saying you may feel differently about it when you're twenty-five."

"No. I won't."

"Let's just drop it," she says finally.

"But—"

"*Drop it.*"

We ride the rest of the way in silence.

During the week I'm home, Dad says very little about the house even when I ask about it, but I can see it's wearing on him.

Rachel picks me up the night before Christmas and we go to the McDonald's drive-thru. We order French fries, Coke, and ice cream cones then eat in the car in the parking lot with the engine on and the heater running.

"I'm sick of college applications," Rachel says, licking her ice cream cone. "Mom nags me about them every night. All I care about is going to the prom with Joey Reynolds, the senior class president. Thing is, I think he's sleeping with this girl I hate on the cheerleading squad, Nina Hopper. She's not even pretty."

"Are you sure?" I ask.

"No, just rumors," she says. I feel so far behind.

"This guy at school, Jesse Evans, kissed me a few weeks ago by the vending machines at school," I say, dipping a fry into my ice cream.

"There are straight guys at your school?" she asks in surprise.

"Yes," I say defensively.

"Do you like him?" she asks. "Is he your boyfriend?"

"No," I say finally, realizing just how much I don't know what's going on in my own life, and also that

I can't imagine Jesse as my boyfriend, no matter how gorgeous he is. "We don't really have time for boyfriends. I'm not even sure what I'm doing next year. My mom is making me send in at least three college applications, but I have to get into a ballet company, Rachel. Getting into BNY is the only thing I care about."

"You've wanted it forever, ever since kindergarten I think," she says. "You're the only person I know who knows what they want to be when they grow up."

After we finish the food we drive by Nina Hopper's house to see if Joey Reynolds' car is in the driveway. It isn't, but Rachel tries to talk me into toilet-papering her house anyway. I feel lame when I tell her I need to get home. This stuff just doesn't seem important to me anymore, even though Rachel used to be my best friend. My dad reassures me that the one thing Rachel and I will always have in common is our whole lives. True as that may be, seeing her makes me realize how much I've changed in the last year and a half.

Chapter 10

In January, the company auditions begin along with the buildup for the spring workshop performances, which I'll perform in this year now that I'm in the advanced class. The pressure to get a job is in each correction, glance, and thought. Almost everyone in my class is a senior, and we won't be welcome at ballet school next year. Our life goals will shatter or materialize in the next few months.

The stress distracts me from the weird feelings I had before the break, and socially things start to feel more like normal. Tyler and I start talking, casually, and going together in *pas de deux* class again.

"Jesse dumped Nicole on the phone over winter break," Tyler whispers to me as we wait behind Jesse and Hilary to dance the *adagio*.

"I heard," I say, pleased that he's being so friendly. "Nicole has been giving a lot of drama lately in class. She keeps sitting down saying her back hurts, but she seems more depressed than injured. I think Hilary's enjoying it."

"I hope she gets over it soon," Tyler says, and I can feel his breath on my neck as I look at us in the mirror. "Jesse isn't worth it." He takes my hand and leads me forward. I step into a high *arabesque*. Our eyes lock as he faces me, pivoting me on one toe in a perfect circle. His partnering is more sensitive than ever. We look at each other while we dance, and when we can't see each other, I'm so conscious of Tyler I can see him in my mind's eye. We're better than we ever were before. I feel connected to him, physically and mentally. This is how partnering is supposed to be. I feel happy and energized, like I could dance with him forever.

"Anna," Jesse says, reaching past me to grab a yogurt in the cafeteria at the end of a particularly long day. "Maybe you can get Tyler to come out. I want someone to go with me to the movies tonight." I notice Tyler is in the check out line already.

"Oh," I say, barely glancing at him. "I don't think so."

"Come on," Jesse says, flashing his charming grin.

"I'm going straight to bed after dinner," I say lamely. "Thanks though." I pick my tray to go over to the soda fountain but he blocks my path.

"There are other things in life besides ballet," Jesse says. "What is wrong with you people?"

"Geez," I say. "I know there are other things, but I'm busy, and Tyler can make up his own mind."

"Why doesn't anyone want to have fun around here?" he asks. "I know *you* like hanging out with me."

"We're just busy right now," I say, glaring at him. "Auditions and workshop are coming up. I'm sure you're thinking about jobs too."

"Not really," he says. "There's always college if BNY doesn't take me. It's only ballet."

I stare at him, shocked. "It means a lot to me," I say.

"Well," he says rudely. "Excuse me."

I shake my head, and after a moment I move past him to get my drink. When I hear him walk away I let out a sigh of relief. I feel tired of him.

I go to a professional photographer to get my résumé pictures taken right after I return from winter break. The photographer takes dozens of headshots and different full body pictures of me in classical poses: *arabesque, passé, grande jété*. I study the negatives with fascination when I see what I really look like. The photos aren't exactly what I expected, and looking at them makes me feel like I don't know myself at all. I can see the corrections I get in class far more clearly: my shoulders are up and my back is swayed in many of the shots, and I look younger and far more fragile than I imagined. And in way I didn't expect, I'm beautiful in an individual and unique way too. All I can do is pray that Victor Caldwell, Bruce Pollock, Charles Diamond, William Mason, or another director will offer me a job.

Every girl in my class takes the auditions in January and February for San Francisco, Los Angeles, Miami, and Seattle, the other four big companies that perform Roizman ballets. The directors are all former dancers with BNY. SBNY and NBT never hold open auditions; they don't need to because they're based in New York.

The auditions are agonizing. They make cuts after *barre* because the studio is too crowded. It's hard enough to stand there and be judged by the top directors in the country, and when it's my turn to dance I'm so nervous I feel like I'm going to vomit. Even though the auditions force everyone into an emotional frenzy, they provide very few answers. Charles Diamond from Ballet San Francisco takes my résumé, Marie's, and Nicole's at the end of the class. We wait every day for a call or a letter, and no letter comes. Los Angeles sends me a rejection in the mail three weeks after the audition. Miami puts us through the whole audition, and then announces that they aren't hiring. At the Seattle audition they announce at the beginning that they won't even consider girls under five-foot five, so I walk out without dancing a step.

Every day we wait, hoping that a director will think of us a week after the audition, change his mind, decide to call or write. But there is nothing except empty mailboxes, silent phones, and increasing anxiety. The competition has become so fierce that we can barely look at each other.

Only two, Nicole and Faye, receive job offers out of my entire class of fifteen. Marie and I nearly die when Charles Diamond offers Nicole an apprenticeship with Ballet San Francisco. We were at the summer program last year, and he's never seen Nicole before. She's not even interested in his company.

"I'm not taking it," Nicole tells Charlie in line in front of me in the cafeteria. "I'm getting into BNY."

"Of course," Charlie says. "You're the best dancer in the class."

I bite my tongue, turn around, and walk out of the cafeteria. I feel so discouraged and jealous. I'm angry that success is so unfair.

The job offer Faye receives surprises everyone. She's a willowy, quiet girl who doesn't live in the dorms. William Mason offers her an apprenticeship with Los Angeles Ballet Theatre. It's unexpected. I felt like Faye was one of the girls the teachers tended to overlook, and I think she felt that way too, because she doesn't even ask the school about getting into BNY, she just accepts the LABT offer on the spot. I'm happy for her, but also jealous. Getting a real job in a good company is such a big deal. Winning the lottery seems to be easier than becoming a professional dancer.

I need a decent part in workshop desperately, and so does Marie. Sometimes the directors that come to the performances in June notice someone onstage they didn't notice in the audition. Those performances will be our last chance to get a job before we graduate from high school, and if I don't get a job this year, I can kiss my ballet dream goodbye. I'm eighteen now. Nineteen is too old.

Because the next year is so undecided, I'm somewhat relieved that Mom made me apply to college, even though I know I don't want to go.

Every day I check my mailbox obsessively for letters on ballet company letterhead, and to my surprise, I receive acceptance packets from Fordham University, and the University of Chicago on full scholarship. Columbia and Stanford send rejection letters. I know college is important, but I already know what I want to be when I grow up. I've known since I was a little girl. College would be a waste of time.

Jeff Talroy uses his weekly *pas de deux* class as an audition for his workshop ballet. Tyler and I finish a *pirouette* combination with a clean triple right in front of him and can't help smiling.

The class is tense, and Jeff tells people who to partner with so he can see which girls and boys look good dancing together. He leads Marie over to Jesse and asks them to do a complicated combination traveling across the floor.

As Jeff gestures to Inessa, the pianist, Jesse positions himself in the back corner behind Marie. Her sticklike legs scissor three times with precision into a split as Jesse supports her back and waist, boosting her flight higher and farther with each split jump. Marie steps forward on her right leg, into a piqué arabesque, while her left leg extends high behind her. Jesse places his right hand on her right hip and his left hand under her raised left leg. Bending his knees, he hoists her high over his head and straightens his arms. Walking in a full circle, he parades with her to the center of the room. With bravado, he bends his knees and elbows slightly, and with a slight forward rotation in the wrist, tosses Marie into thin air. She straightens her right leg next to her left, executing a full horizontal flip in the air at breakneck speed. We all know Jesse is supposed to catch her waist and leg then lower her to a fish dive with her nose pointing at the floor.

But Jesse is busy looking at himself in the mirror rather than at Marie, and when he tosses her he pushes her a few inches too far away from him.

BAM. Like the sound of a bass drum, a dull thud fills the studio as Marie hits the floor flat on her back. Her piercing scream fills the studio.

The pianist stops abruptly and silence fills the room. Everyone is frozen in shocked silence as Jesse bends down to look into Marie's pain-contorted face. I push my way through the gathering circle of dancers and crouch at Marie's side.

"What happened?" Jeff asks.

Slowly, Marie's eyes focus and she tries to sit up in the center of the circle. She falls back hard, clutching her sides as her head hits the floor again.

"Don't move, Marie," I say.

"My back," Marie says. "Something snapped in my back." I exchange a panic-stricken look with Jeff.

Jeff looks genuinely worried as he gestures to the pianist. "Go immediately to the office, Inessa, and tell them to call an ambulance. Tell the new secretary to call Dr. Westover and ask him to meet Marie at the ER at St. Luke's. Call up to the dorm office too and let them know what happened."

"I'm so sorry, Marie," Jesse says weakly. "I didn't mean to…I thought I could catch you."

She doesn't acknowledge him. "This can't be happening," Marie says. Her usually pale face has turned white. Tears pour down her cheeks.

I feel sick to my stomach. I hope Marie's back is just tweaked, but she keeps moaning. She can't have a serious injury now. The auditions are basically over and she doesn't have a job. If the teachers get the impression this is serious, they'll count her out of workshop. Everything will be over if she can't dance for the next few months. She's already eighteen. It would be the end.

Jeff squats and puts his hand on her shoulder. "It's going to be okay," he says.

Marie looks up into his eyes. "No. I don't think it is," she says.

"It was an accident," Jesse says, backing away. "I'm so sorry…" He looks scared.

I feel so horrible for her, but all I can think is that I'm so glad it wasn't me. I'm so glad it wasn't me. I'm a terrible friend, but I'm so glad it wasn't me.

There doesn't seem to be anything good to say, and the next few minutes feel like hours until the paramedics arrive. Very gently, with an air of polished expertise, they move Marie onto a stretcher. She continues to whimper. We stare in somber silence as they carry her out of the room.

"Class," Jeff says, "that's enough for today." He hurries out of the room and Jesse runs after him, still trying to explain. We sigh collectively in relief. Everyone looks dazed as they trickle out of the studio.

I think about how Marie moved all the way from France and left her family and worked herself to death just to have it all come down to this. Her parents even sold their *house*.

I visit Marie a few times in the hospital over the next two weeks. Her parents fly in and she has surgery. The doctors put a steel rod in her back—and tell her she'll never dance again. She's lucky she isn't paralyzed and there will be months of rehab ahead. Eventually her mom tells me it would be better if I don't visit for a while. Marie is sick of seeing me because I reminder her of everything she lost.

They post the casting for workshop a few days later.

"Congratulations," Faye says as I push my way through the crowd in front of the board.

I scan the list of the *corps de ballet*, which includes most of my class, but I don't see my name anywhere. I feel a rush of panic that I'm not even going to be in workshop at all.

Then I see it. I have to blink. I rub my eyes, but it's still there. My name, next to the principal roles in two of the four ballets on the program: *Waltz* and *Fire*. "I can't believe it." Nicole and Hilary are also learning the lead in *Fire*, and Hilary is my alternate in *Waltz*.

When I turn around, I find myself looking into a sea of troubled faces staring up at the board. I can feel the desperation. Workshop casting is almost as crucial as the company auditions. It's the most honest indication we get of what the school thinks of us.

Because of the casting, I realize I'll have the best possible remaining shot at a job because of these performances, and I feel happy. All the artistic directors will be there. Victor Caldwell will finally see me perform.

I'm excited, but after a few hours of processing the news, the casting also feels arbitrary. I thought I worked hard last year and the school didn't like me. I'm still the same body with the same work ethic. At the core I haven't changed, and I wonder what happened. A lot of the girls in my class worked as hard as I did this year, and they're only getting one or two small roles in the *corps de ballet*. Jeff Talroy's piece doesn't even have a female lead.

Marie avoids my calls after the workshop casting goes up. I keep calling since I can't visit her in the hospital, but it's useless. I don't want to let go of her so easily. I'm frustrated that she's pushed me away, and no matter what happens to either of us, I can't believe we won't be a part of each other's lives forever.

Workshop preparations begin the following week, and the atmosphere is different because of it. We all have a clear purpose and defined roles in it. The jockeying for position is over, at least temporarily now that casting has been decided.

Waltz rehearsals are tough. We start by having separate rehearsals from the *corps de ballet* to learn the principal roles, and Madame Sivenko, who used to dance the principal in *Waltz* herself, teaches us the steps.

Qi is my partner for *Waltz*, which is comforting. He's quiet and easy to work with, and I trust him. Sometimes we have trouble because he doesn't speak much English and he's very shy, but he knows how to partner. A lot of the guys are more concerned with how they look than with making the girl look good, which is kind of the kiss of death for making partnering work. Luckily Qi isn't like that at all.

Hilary and Charlie are partners, and because they're both dramatic and temperamental, we waste a large amount of rehearsal time waiting for them to stop fighting. They're a contrast to us. The louder they are the quieter we become.

Madame Sivenko has us watch the video, which shows a young version of her flying across the stage like a dragonfly. She may be a cruel teacher, but she was an amazing dancer. I can still see the shadow of quality in the way she tilts her head or gestures with her arms, even though she hasn't danced a ballet in at least twenty years.

"*Waltz* is like high impact aerobics," Madame Sivenko says, talking over the video as we watch. "The footwork is fast and you need to have lots of energy, even when you get tired. Hilary and Anna, you only have a three-minute rest during the entire twelve-minute ballet. The rest of the time it's just go go go."

In class we always get to stop in between combinations, so while my muscles are strong and my technique is good, I actually don't have a lot of stamina, something that becomes very clear the first time we run the whole ballet. Hilary isn't much better, even though she refuses to commiserate. By the end we're both huffing and puffing like old ladies. I feel like it's a wake-up call. I have a long way to go before I'll be able to dance this full out all the way through at a performance level. Right now I feel like I look like a sloppy, tired mess, even though I'm giving it everything I have.

Nicole, Jesse, Hilary, Jamal, Tyler and I all stand by the door looking nervous at the first *Fire* rehearsal. I feel so lucky to be here.

Vivienne comes in with a clipboard. "Anna, you'll dance with Tyler," she says, and I'm relieved. Tyler is a good match physically, I know we dance well together, and our styles are complementary. Charlie is a bad partner and he's too tall and lanky for me. Jesse is too broad and muscular compared to how petite I am.

Tyler scoots over to me. "Hey," he whispers. "Let's stand in the center." He takes my hand and leads me right to the center of the room. I never stand in the center during class, and a huge knot starts forming in my stomach. It feels strange to be dancing with him after the weirdness of the past few months, even though recently we've warmed up to each other again. I'm still trying to figure out what our relationship is exactly. I feel sensitive about any interaction with him, and the promise of working closely with him on something so important to me rattles my nerves, but makes me excited too.

Jesse stands with his arms crossed over his chest on the other side of the room. He seems like he'd rather be somewhere else. Vivienne puts him with Nicole and they both look unhappy about it. Jamal doesn't look any more thrilled to be put with Hilary, and I guess he's thinking about Marie.

A petite, dark-haired woman in her fifties walks into the room. She isn't wearing a drop of makeup, but she's beautiful. Her body is slender with long legs and she moves with athletic grace. Even though she's wearing a jogging suit and sneakers, she's so magnetic a light seems to shine out of her in every direction. Vivienne walks over to her and they shake hands. I recognize her.

"Oh, my God. That's Stacy Hannah."

"They didn't warn us," Tyler says. "Wow." We look at each other and I think of when he first said we should dance *Fire* together almost 2 years ago.

Vivienne leads Stacy to the center of the room. "I'm honored to introduce Stacy Hannah to you," Vivienne says. "We're fortunate she's willing to take time away from her family to come in and teach you the *pas de deux.* As you know, Roizman choreographed *Fire* specifically for her."

Stacy Hannah scans the room while Vivienne talks, making eye contact with each of us. She's been retired for almost twenty years and still lives in Manhattan. Catching sight of Stacy Hannah is news because when she retired she famously said, "I think I'm ready to start my life now." She's never around.

"They're all yours," Vivienne says to her, sitting down in a chair. Vivienne looks just as curious as the rest of us.

"Good," Stacy says. She clasps her hands together. "Thanks for having me, Vivienne." Her eyes are like bullets, examining us. "When Nicholas choreographed *Fire*—I'll date myself but I think it was close to thirty years ago now—we couldn't believe the stuff he asked us to do. William used to say it gave him the same rush as skydiving. I loved it more and more every time we danced it."

"You're going to practice it a lot before June," Vivienne says.

I smile and Stacy looks right at me but doesn't smile back.

"So, before we start, a few things," Stacy says. "Because the choreography is unconventional it can look like improvisation to the audience, so you have to be deliberate. The *pas de deux* is often described as a representation of the complexity of a romantic relationship. You must learn to trust each other. Men, your partner needs to know you'll be there to catch her when she takes all those risks: falling, jumping across the stage, you know what I mean. I was so lucky to have William."

My eyes move from my own reflection to Tyler's, standing behind me, watching Stacy. He's fixated on her, but then his eyes shift and I jump when I realize he's watching *me* in the glass.

The more I dance these days the less I speak. It drives me crazy that I can't seem to communicate well with my friends or family anymore, and I wonder if dancing with Tyler will magically bring him closer to me again. Maybe I can't communicate with anyone. Ballet is how I speak my feelings and intentions, and I feel like there's so much more truth in what people do than in what they say. Movement doesn't lie. I feel like genuine intention in a gesture is what makes it beautiful.

We spend the next two hours with Stacy Hannah practicing the most difficult aspects of the *pas de deux*, creating just the right tension in our grip on each other to allow me to kick my legs, turn, jump, fall, and fly across the room with Tyler's support. His hands are all over my waist, my hands, my ribs, and my legs. He cradles me in his arms, lifts me up off the floor, and catches me as I fall. Our bodies move naturally together.

"Good you two," Stacy says to us as we execute one of the more difficult lifts successfully for the first time. We're the first couple to get it right. I smile at Tyler, but he's looking past me at our image in the mirror, and I feel a rush of frustration at how difficult it can be to connect with someone, even someone I care about a lot.

Waltz rehearsals become intense. Madame Sivenko makes each cast run the ballet all the way through twice, and because we take turns it begins to feel like Hilary and I are competing with each other. Her presence pushes me not to give in to my exhaustion, but it also gives Madame Sivenko plenty of opportunities to compare us to each other.

"Did you notice how nicely Hilary runs on for her variation, Anna?" Madame Sivenko shouts at me without ever taking her eyes off of Hilary dancing, as I stand on the side of the room during Hilary's run-thru.

I do my best not to cringe. Qi glances at me from across the room and I know he senses my frustration. At least Charlie and Hilary struggle through the partnering sequences, and Madame Sivenko is always telling them to watch *us*.

Hilary comes up to me at the end of rehearsal. "Will you go over the end of the variation with me?" she asks. "I missed the rehearsal when we learned the counts and I'm having trouble with the phrasing."

I'm irritated that Hilary missed the rehearsal, because I know she has a Juilliard boyfriend now and has been telling Madame Sivenko she has tendonitis in order to get out of rehearsing to spend time with him. When she misses rehearsal I have to dance her run-thru with Charlie, which I hate because not only is Charlie careless and clumsy, he blames me for everything that goes wrong and he smells like pot. And I think Hilary's lazy and doesn't think she needs to run the ballet twice, even though she can barely get through the entire piece. I go over the counts with her several times anyway.

Afterwards, she walks over to pick up her bag on her way out the door. "Thanks Anna," she says. "Now if I mess it up, I can blame you."

I stand there fuming as Hilary walks out of the studio. I feel like one day we're just going to claw each other's eyes out.

The *Fire* rehearsals put Tyler and me back on speaking terms. I'm happy that things are better between us, and I realize I look forward to the rehearsals as much for the time I spend with him as for the dancing. I missed his edginess and humor. He always used to make me feel good about myself. Our partnership feels safe and comforting and at the same time pushes me to try harder.

"It's Anna, right?" Stacy Hannah asks after we've been rehearsing for several weeks.

I nod and she walks closer, making eye contact with me.

"We have a similar body type," she says. "You're back is very flexible, which makes that backbend look great, but you need to hold your stomach to come back up."

"Okay," I say, pleased to get a correction from her. Tyler dips me again. As we come up I concentrate on engaging my stomach muscles and I nearly fly out of his arms.

"Hmm," Stacy says. "Don't overcompensate for her," she tells Tyler. Jamal, Hilary, Nicole, and Jesse stop practicing to watch us.

We try again. I can feel him subtly applying her adjustment, and this time it works perfectly.

"Dammmmmmm," Jamal says supportively.

"Better," Stacy says. Tyler and I nod at her, and we both make a mental note to apply the correction from now on every time we dance the *pas de deux*. "I think that's enough for today," she says. "I'll see you on Thursday."

We applaud. I'm sad the rehearsal is over. I felt uncomfortable at the beginning about standing front center in these rehearsals, but actually, Tyler was smart. Stacy spends more time with us than either of the other two couples. It almost makes me wonder if I've been putting myself at a disadvantage by standing in the back row for so long.

I wish I could talk to Stacy Hannah outside the studio. I'd love to hear some of her stories, and to know what she's like as a person. I feel desperate for a mother figure, or at least someone who would understand what I'm going through and offer some comfort or support. But there's no one.

Chapter 11

The days fly by because of all the rehearsals, and its May before I knew April even arrived. Marie finally agrees to see me. She's out of the hospital, and her mom moves her out of the dorms into an apartment. Her mom plans to stay the rest of the school year and bring Marie her schoolwork and take her to therapy. That way Marie can still graduate on schedule.

I walk over to her apartment that evening feeling nervous. Marie hasn't been to ballet class in two months. I've asked Jamal about Marie a few times because he's the only person she talks to anymore, but he won't say much.

We sit and her mom brings us each a piece of cake. Marie seems like a different person. The old Marie wouldn't touch dessert if it were the last food on earth.

"Tell me about rehearsals," Marie says after a few moments of silence.

I look at her, trying to decide if this is too difficult, but she's asking. I'm afraid she'll see how guilty I still feel. And I'm mad at her for withdrawing. It's not my fault she got injured. I want to be friends outside of ballet; I just hope it's possible. I feel like we had a connection because of who we are as people, not just as dancers, and I'm frustrated that ballet seems to be driving us apart.

"*Waltz* rehearsals kind of suck because after we learned it Hilary started skipping all the time," I say. "She says she has tendonitis, which is an exaggeration. I know she's off with that Juilliard actor. Madame Sivenko doesn't even get mad. I end up rehearsing with both casts."

"Does she take it for granted that she'll get in to BNY?" Marie asks. "Nicole's the one I think will get in. Hilary's not a sure thing. Victor hasn't shown any interest in her."

"I don't know," I say, disliking the thought of either Hilary or Nicole getting in to BNY.

"You have to admit Nicole is good," she says. She tucks her blonde hair behind her ears.

I shrug, reluctant to admit it. "What about you? How's your back?" I finally ask.

"It is better, thanks," she says. "I'm going to therapy all the time. I'm still miles away from normal though."

"You'll get there."

"Have you talked to Jesse?" I ask.

"Yes. It's fine. It was an accident. He feels bad enough."

"I would be so angry."

"Whatever," she says, and I can tell she wants to drop it.

"What are you going to do in June?" I ask, trying to change the subject.

She makes lines with her fork through the chocolate cake. "Well," she says. "I will be here doing therapy for the summer, but then I am going to Columbia in the fall."

"Columbia University?" College?

"Yes," she says quietly. She shrugs. "Everyone in BNY is miserable anyway," she adds. I wonder if she means it, or if she's just scared she won't be able to dance again.

"But they're in the best ballet company in the world," I say.

"Well it's not like I have a choice," she snaps. "I think I want to go to law school."

"You want to be a lawyer?" How has she already developed a new dream? Then I realize, maybe it's because she doesn't have a choice.

"Then I can force directors to earn a special degree," she says. So her new dream is still deeply rooted in the old one. "They should have a background in psychology and child development. Ballet companies are too much like dictatorships."

I raise my eyebrows, but I think I know what she means.

She leans forward, her green eyes glowing. "Seriously," she says. "Athletes can do college at the same time they do their sport, and most of them earn enough money to support themselves later when they are old and the body breaks down. And they get to be heroes."

"But we're *artists*, Marie, it's not the same. We're supposed to suffer." I didn't realize her injury had made her so bitter. Did she blame SBNY for her fall?

"You're so naïve," she says. "The ballet world is sick. It does not give us time or support to develop other interests. I have realized since my injury that maybe it is not so noble to give up so much for the sake of art. We convince ourselves that all we need is ballet. What about when we turn forty? There is no pension or job security in American ballet. We will never even be technically qualified for many entry-level jobs outside dance."

"Why would dancers want jobs outside of dance? You know it's like we have a calling, Marie." I feel like she's personally attacking me. Her criticism feels like betrayal.

"Oh please!" she says. "Get over yourself. Most people never see what dancers do. They care a lot more for the New York Knicks than for Ballet New York. Who will take care of the dancers? The directors cannot worry about individuals. It is all they can do to keep their companies from going under."

I know she's hurting, but I can't believe she's saying all this.

We sit there, not looking at each other. Who does she think she is? One injury and she's now better than the whole ballet world? I thought we could still be friends, but now I realize it's impossible.

Besides, ballet politics will only change when the world cares more for the artist than the product. That's never going to happen, because human beings die, and art can live forever. Paintings go in museums. Movies stay on film. Books lie on shelves. Music goes on CD.

The problem is that ballet only exists when people dance. When the dancers leave, the ballet is gone.

Videotape doesn't capture the essence of a ballet performance. A camera can only focus on a small part of what happens on the stage. Film loses the patterns in choreography, arms, legs, faces, depth perception, and the element of live performance. It's impossible to write down every intention and movement a choreographer envisioned.

I don't think anything can preserve a living soul in motion.

"Face it Anna, most ballet directors and teachers only care about impossible standards for weight and body type," Marie says. "And most of us kill ourselves trying to achieve it."

"I don't want to talk about this anymore." I stand up and walk out of the restaurant. Marie follows me. We walk home in silence.

I feel like it's horrible that career decisions are based on bodies, not on spirits. Ballet demands that we put our spirits out for judgment every day. The contradiction between the need for spirit and the disrespect for individuals traps us in a hopeless paradox.

Maybe ballet is a dying art form.

Who will dance if all the ballet hearts are broken?

Fire rehearsals become more and more intense. I find myself thinking about the steps as I fall asleep, in my dreams, and during every spare moment of the day. Jen shakes me awake in the middle of the night on more than one occasion because I'm talking out loud. I keep practicing in my sleep and kicking the wall so hard I wake her up.

Stacy Hannah's voice and eyes are in my head all the time. She wants something so particular, something beyond words. She focuses on Tyler and me more than the others in rehearsals. Vivienne often jumps in and gets her to correct Nicole and Jesse or Hilary and Jamal, but Tyler and I are the favorites. I want to embody her vision.

After a few weeks, Stacy decides that each couple should run the entire *pas de deux* alone. Jesse and Nicole volunteer to go first, and Hilary, Jamal, and Tyler sit down together in a group on the side. I stand in the back corner to mark through the steps. Vivienne sits in the corner, watching silently.

They take their places and Stacy signals to the pianist. After practicing the individual lifts and particular steps separately so many times, it's a new experience for us to connect them. It's like the end of practicing a note and finally singing the song. The choreography is no longer a flash of beautiful pose here, a good *pirouette* there; it's an extended experience in time. Jesse expertly guides Nicole through the *pas de deux*, and it's amazing to see it take shape. Even though they seem to hate each other ever since their short fling, their emotions add chemistry to their dancing.

Stacy lets them run the whole thing all the way through without stopping. It's a traditional *pas de deux*: the adagio first, when the man and woman dance together at a slower pace, then the man's variation, a bravura solo where he jumps and turns and performs athletic tricks that make the audience applaud, followed by the woman's variation, which highlights delicate footwork on pointe, and finally the coda, or finale, when they dance together again, repeating steps that have become themes carried over from the adagio, but speeding up. The coda includes the man performing turning leaps around the stage and the woman executing thirty-two difficult *fouettés*, consecutive whip turns on one leg. At the end she runs and leaps across the stage into his arms and he catches her a centimeter away from the floor. Each pose and movement that we've broken down and analyzed is suddenly integrated into the choreography; not just a vocabulary anymore, but a language.

My eyes are glued on Nicole, who is limber and beautiful and looks great in the part. Jesse partners her expertly. I watch the way her body moves and think about how to apply it to myself. It's intimidating to see her tackling the role, but if she can do it, I can do it.

"Next?" Stacy says after she gives Jesse and Nicole a few brief corrections. Tyler looks at Hilary and Jamal as if to say, "We'll be going last, so you're on." They stand up and Hilary shoots Tyler an angry look. She wanted to be last. Jamal doesn't seem to care.

Jesse walks over to the side by me and I instinctively move away from him. Tyler glances up and seems to notice. I walk to the back of the studio away from both of them.

Hilary and Jamal have more difficulty when they run the *pas de deux*. The partnering doesn't seem to work for them. Their timing with each other is off. He looks awkward and she looks irritated, and their frustrated attitude makes them look bad, even though they both have great technique and beautiful bodies. It's just as interesting to see all the things that don't work for them as it was to see Jesse and Nicole do everything right. Vivienne looks frustrated, and she keeps glancing at Stacy Hannah to check her reaction. When Jamal and Hilary finish, Stacy goes over a few of the trouble spots with them, but it doesn't seem like a problem easy to fix. They don't partner well together.

"Okay, Anna. Jesse," Stacy says. Tyler comes over to me and takes my hand, leading me out onto the floor. I'm excited to dance with him.

I strike the opening pose, my profile flat to the audience, looking into the wing with one leg in front of the other on pointe. Tyler steps behind me, his profile also to the audience, looking in the same direction. He takes my left hand and puts his right hand underneath my other arm to give me support.

On the first note, I bend my left leg, still on pointe, and let my right leg fly out behind me in a powerful kick. We move through the choreography, punctuating the Stravinsky music with our bodies. I become warmer as we go. We both watch our reflections carefully in the mirror. Tyler's face is as intense as my own, and the music seems to dictate our feelings and our timing.

The adagio ends with a difficult turn. I spin away by pushing against Tyler's arm and whipping my leg around before I pull in and try to spin as many times as I can. It's a turn we've messed up repeatedly, but during this run through we're warm and charged up and we nail it. I hit a perfect triple and sustain the ending. Jamal whistles as I run off the floor.

Tyler dances his variation while I bend over on the side, trying to catch my breath. His solo doesn't last nearly long enough, and I'm back on for my variation before I've gotten my breathing under control. I fly through the steps, counting to stay precisely on the music. Hilary and Charlie watch me carefully from the side. I'm most aware of Stacy and Vivienne's eyes, but I can't help seeing Jesse studying me from the front.

My variation ends and we repeat the opening, moving towards the final moments in the *pas de deux*. Tyler's touch feels natural and he helps me to dance better. I can feel his exhaustion as if it's my own, but it's a good feeling, a team feeling. We push each other mentally, willing ourselves to the end. His sweat runs down across my skin and I can feel his heart beating. I run towards him to take a flying leap, and when I hit the air I'm so incredibly *alive*. He catches me and pulls me back out of the jump, abruptly stopping my forward motion. My nose nearly hits the floor as my legs wrap backwards around his head. We hit the final pose just as the music ends.

There's a moment of silence. For some reason my eyes wander over to Hilary. She looks furious, and I quickly move my eyes away.

"Good," Stacy says. "Let's talk about a few things." She walks over to us. "Show me the pull-away." Tyler takes my hands and we go back to one of the trickier parts, when he holds my hands and pulls away from me as I stand on pointe on my right toe and stretch my left leg to the sky in a vertical split. Stacy coaches us into being more risky and off-balance. The moment is immediately better.

The blood is pounding in my ears and I'm sweating like mad, but I feel good. This role is right for me. I remember when I thought I'd never be able to dance something so complicated, and now I know I can.

"That's enough for today," Stacy says. "Good."

We clap and I walk over to the side to take off my shoes. Tyler sits down next to me and pulls a towel out of his bag to wipe his face. We're so connected when we dance, but as soon as the piece ends, it's a letdown when the spell breaks. But still, I feel on top of the world and extremely close to him. We worked hard for this, and I know we danced better than we ever have before.

Stacy Hannah and Vivienne leave the room, whispering. Nicole and Hilary are talking by the door, and when Vivienne disappears, Nicole turns to go.

"I need a cigarette," Jesse says, leaning on the *barre* to take off his ballet slippers. He walks over to Tyler. "Wanna go smoke?"

"No, thanks," Tyler says, not looking at him, and there's something in the tone of his voice that makes me look closer at them.

"Come on," Jesse says, and he smacks Tyler's butt with one of his shoes, in a way that makes me feel uncomfortable.

"No," Tyler says loudly, flinching, and all of a sudden, for the first time, I wonder, is Jesse gay? That might explain some of the awkwardness between us, and why I can't understand where he's coming from so much of the time.

Hilary interrupts my train of thought by walking over and squatting down so she can whisper in my ear. "Anna," she says, "great job today."

I snap my head up in surprise. "Oh! Thanks," I say, startled. I feel a surprising rush of sympathy for her, but when I glance up I see her eyes are filled with venom.

"Just remember, it's not over yet," Hilary whispers. She smiles a wicked smile, and turns and walks out of the room. Jesse follows behind her. I feel anger boiling up inside of me at both of them.

Jamal throws his warmers into his bag and stands up. He seems upset over the rehearsal too. "Marie should be doing this instead of Hilary," he mutters as he walks out of the studio. The thought of Marie makes me sad. I feel like I've lost one of my best friends.

I stand up and meet Tyler's eyes. I feel scared and confused. All the joy of dancing has already melted away. Tyler moves closer to me, as if he can read my mind, and it feels perfectly natural when he pulls me into a hug. I pull him close and bury my face in his chest, not caring how sweaty and gross we are. The sound of his heartbeat makes me feel better. We stay that way for a long time, and he holds me tight until I'm ready to let go. My hair is frizzed and my face is splotchy when I glance in the mirror, but he doesn't seem to care, and when we walk out of the studio together I laugh at one of his jokes. Later, when I crawl into bed that night, I fall asleep thinking about how tenderly we embraced.

Chapter 12

I go to a podiatrist in a brownstone on the Upper East Side to have the corns removed from between my little toes. They've been killing me for weeks. I can't bear to put it off for any longer and I don't want to be in pain for the performances, which are less than a month away.

As I'm leaving the office, I open the door and find myself standing face to face with none other than Stacy Hannah.

"Anna," she says, her voice warm. "Hello."

"Hi." I'm thrilled she recognizes me outside the studio. She's wearing a blue sundress and sandals, and she's even more striking outside of the ballet environment, on a lovely tree-lined street in the real world.

"Are you okay?" she asks.

"Me?" I ask. "Oh, yes, yes, I'm fine. Just had to get some corns removed."

"Ah," she says. Her eyes are just as penetrating, studying me. We stand there for moment in awkward silence. "May I ask," she says, "what your plans are for next year?"

"Next year? I…well I really need a job."

"Have they said anything to you about BNY?" she asks.

"No." I'm embarrassed to admit it.

"I see," she says. "Did you audition for Los Angeles? I would think you'd be just the type of dancer William looks for."

"I auditioned in February and didn't get in. William wasn't at the audition though. Lili, the ballet mistress, and Simone, the resident choreographer, ran the audition."

"I see," she says. "Well, something will work out. You're looking good in *Fire*. You have a special quality. It's rare at this school, especially considering how they try to strip away your individuality. Don't lose that personality in your dancing. It will set you apart."

"Thank you! I mean…thank you so much. You just made my whole day. My whole year, actually." *Yes.*

She smiles. "I won't be at any more of the rehearsals," she says. "My husband is speaking at a conference in San Francisco and I'm going to be staging *America* for Charles Diamond at Ballet San Francisco, so I won't be back in New York until the end of the summer. I'm so sorry I won't see the workshop performances. You've worked so hard. I'm sure Vivienne will tell me all about it."

"Oh, I didn't realize." I can't believe she's not going to see me onstage. "I'm so sad you'll miss it."

"Don't worry," she says. "I already know you'll be great."

I'm blushing and stammering and all I can say is "thank you."

"Goodbye," she says, and then she disappears into the brownstone, leaving me with my jaw hanging open on the corner of Madison Avenue.

"Anna, I need to speak with you," Vivienne says at the end of *Fire* rehearsal the following week.

Hilary jumps up and scurries out of the studio, which strikes me as odd. It seems like Hilary always wants to be right in the center of anything involving gossip. Jesse and Jamal follow her. Nicole and Tyler stare openly as I walk over to Vivienne.

"Anna," Vivienne say as she places her arm on the piano. "You don't need to come to *Fire* rehearsals anymore. Nicole and Hilary will each have two performances. You're to focus more on *Waltz*."

"I don't understand," I say.

"We're taking you out of *Fire*," she says.

"You're taking me out of *Fire*?" I'm floored.

"Yes, we are." She looks at me with no expression.

I can't believe what I've just heard, and yet I nod. I nod, even though I feel like screaming. I wish they decided this before they let me spend months rehearsing and getting excited. I'd give up *Waltz* in a heartbeat to perform *Fire*. I'm better in it than Hilary. I know I am. Why are they taking me out? Stacy said I looked terrific.

Vivienne picks up her notebook. Her shoulders sag and she lets out a sigh as she walks past me and out the door. My hands start trembling, and I cover my face and take a deep breath to get myself together. When I finally turn around, the studio is empty except for Tyler and Nicole, lingering in the doorway. "What was that about?" Tyler asks.

I pick up my bag and walk to the door. "They took me out."

"Oh," he says, and he looks surprised.

"I can't believe it," I say.

"At least you still have *Waltz*," Nicole says. She unpins her long dark hair and lets it fall to her shoulders.

"I know," I say, wondering why she's still here. She's not my friend.

"Why?" Tyler asks.

"I don't know," I say. "Vivienne said I should focus on *Waltz*. Tyler, we've been talking about dancing this piece together for two years. I can't believe we won't get to perform it." I search his eyes for an answer he doesn't have.

Nicole coughs. "Anna," she says, and I tear my eyes away from Tyler to look at her. What does she want? Isn't this enough of a triumph for her—does she really need to hang around and rub my face in it?

"I think you deserve to know something," Nicole says nervously. Tyler crosses his arms and turns to look at her.

"What?" I ask, sighing.

"Hilary…" she starts, biting her fingernail.

"Hilary?" Tyler asks.

"I think you should know that Hilary's parents donated a million dollars to the school this week," Nicole says, "and they made sure to let Madame Sivenko know how much they'd like to see Hilary have two performances of *Fire*."

I feel like my head might explode in a rush of anger. "Why are you telling me this?" I ask.

"That bitch," Tyler says.

Nicole puts her bag over her shoulder. "That said, you looked better in it than she did," she says. "Everyone knows it. But this isn't about fairy tales. This is the real world. And people do what they have to do to get ahead. I just thought you deserved to know."

"I thought Hilary was your best friend," I say, my eyes filling up.

"I don't have friends," Nicole says. "That's always a mistake." I feel like it has to be a painful thing to say, but she says it with no emotion. She walks out of the room. I don't get her at all.

"Oh my God," I say. "I've never wanted to kill anyone so badly in my life."

Tyler runs a hand through his hair, looking disgusted. I'm so crushed, and angry, I feel like getting on the next plane home to Rock Island.

The world doesn't stop because I've lost my dream role. Instead, everything intensifies as we get closer and closer to the performances. I do the only thing I really can. I throw myself into my role in *Waltz*. The more

I dance *Waltz*, the more I feel like I've been pigeonholed into a certain type of role, because *Waltz* is ideal for a short girl who can jump well. In a way, it's comforting, because I know I'm just that. After about a week, despite my anger, I admit that I'm a little relieved. There's less pressure. I keep telling myself that *Fire* is for someone a little taller, a little sexier, a little….well I don't know. It's just not mine anymore.

I can't talk to my friends about it. Marie is removed from workshop and ballet politics now, and we've drifted so far apart. Jen tells me she's really sorry, but my problems must be so childish to her now that she's been in National Ballet Theatre for almost eight months. Jen never liked to join in my Hilary-hating anyway.

On Sunday of performance week I rush through the cafeteria and grab a quick dinner to eat by myself. No one feels social right now, and I'd rather eat alone and think about *Waltz*. I pick a corner table and hope I won't see anyone.

Jesse walks around the corner and spots me. "This seat taken?" he asks.

I shrug. He doesn't take the cue, and sits down. We eat in silence for a while. I feel as awkward with him as always. There's something about our personalities that just doesn't connect.

"I'm really sorry about *Fire*," he says.

My eyes unexpectedly fill up with tears. "Yeah."

"You looked great in it," he says. "I'm not just saying that."

"Thank you," I say, surprised.

"What are you doing next year?" he asks.

"Good question." I still don't know what I'll do if I don't get in anywhere.

"So you're still hoping to get a job?" he asks.

"I don't really know what I'll do if I don't get into a company," I say honestly. "I'm not ready to go to college, not now. I really want to dance professionally. You're graduating too. Have they said anything to you about BNY? Or are you serious about college?" Even though Jesse's not nearly as good as Tyler, he's improved a lot, and he is dancing the lead role in Jeff Talroy's ballet. BNY need guys. They always need guys.

"I think I have a decent shot at the company," he says.

"Yeah, you probably do," I say. I'm jealous that he has the confidence to say it, and feel myself shutting down towards him.

He shrugs. "Jeff Talroy has been very supportive of me."

"That's great."

"Can I ask you a question?" he asks, and before I can respond he blurts out, "Are you and Tyler together?"

"No," I say, taken by surprise. "Why do you ask?"

"Just wondered," he says. He picks up his tray to go. "See you later."

I watch him walk away, and I'm confused and overwhelmed by emotions I didn't know I had. I'm frustrated that I ever thought Jesse was cute. I can't believe I kissed him, because we're not on the same wavelength at all, and I feel like he has hidden motives I don't fully understand. I'm angrier than ever at Hilary, with whom I never wanted a war, and doesn't deserve to have *Fire*. I miss Marie and I can't believe our friendship has fallen apart. I wonder how I can ever be close to Jen again, when I'm falling more and more behind in ballet while she moves forward. I'm scared of growing up, I miss my mom and dad, and I'm desperate to get a job. Tyler is the last thing on my mind right now.

The weekend of workshop arrives at last. When I see my mom and dad, I'm overwhelmed with emotion. Their physical presence reminds me that I'm not just a dancer. I'm a daughter. So much time has passed in which I've been like a machine, putting dance above everything. I've treated all my personal relationships like they're in the way. I'm exhausted by it. My emotional reaction surprises me, because even though I miss them from time to time, I spend most of my days behaving like my parents don't exist. It drives home how much I pretend I don't need anyone and it isn't true. I need love desperately.

Mom runs up to hug me when I meet them outside the hotel. "You look so grown up," she says, and

I realize I've lived away from them for almost two years. She's more beautiful than I remembered.

I'm already tearing up when Dad puts his arms around me. "Hi, Pumpkin," Dad says. Having them here is so different than when I go home to Rock Island. New York is my world, and this is the first time my parents have come to visit me instead of the other way around. I remember how I snapped at my dad the last time he offered to visit, and I feel bad that I didn't let them come before.

We go to dinner at Fiorello's. My mom is wearing a new green dress, and she's even put on makeup for the occasion. Dad is wearing the same blue jacket he's had since I was a kid. Something about that jacket is so comforting to me. It seems impossible that they were ever apart, or there was ever a time in the universe when they didn't know each other.

I spend the meal telling them all about the ballets they're going to see, about my friends, about what my teachers are like. They listen to me with their full attention. The stress temporarily floats away as we become a family again.

On opening night, Faye sits next to me and we check each other's makeup in the dressing room. I'm wearing blue sweat pants over my pink tights with a matching blue zip up jacket to keep warm while I get ready. The performances are in the Juilliard theatre adjacent to SBNY, which is small but cozy and respectable. Faye doesn't seem nervous the way I am, and I feel like it's because she already has her job with Los Angeles Ballet Theatre. I'm grateful to be near someone calm.

Madame Sivenko surprises all of us when she appears in the dressing room.

"Hi girls," she says. "Where's Anna?" She looks around and spots me. Her blonde hair, bobbed and sleek, is the exact color of her silk dress.

"Hi Madame Sivenko." I wave across the room. Everyone is watching her, and me.

"I'm here to pin in your hairpiece for *Waltz*," she says. Hilary glances up from applying her makeup across the room. I feel a stab of anger that I'm dancing *Waltz* and Hilary's dancing *Fire* tonight, and I'm grateful Madame Sivenko has sought me out. Madame Sivenko comes over to me and picks up the headpiece, a cap of tiny rhinestones, sitting by my makeup case.

"Okay," I say. "I'm just finishing my makeup." She watches me apply a deep red color to my lips. The others turn their attention back to the mirrors.

When I'm done, Madame Sivenko examines my French twist with her typical eagle eye. I watch her in the mirror while she arranges every single rhinestone as if it came straight from Van Cleef and Arpels.

"I loved dancing this ballet," she says to me. She nods in satisfaction with her handiwork. "Hand me some pins." I hand her a bobby pin and she jams it into my hair as if my head is a pincushion. It's all I can do not to visibly wince, but I let her pin in the whole thing to her liking, certain my scalp must be bleeding.

"Thank you," I tell her.

"Yes, well," she says, "it's not like *I* get to go out there anymore. Besides, you remind me of myself sometimes. Short, you know."

There's an audible sigh in the dressing room when she leaves.

"*Merde*," I say to wish Faye good luck when she stands up to go downstairs. She smiles. Faye has a quiet quality that calms my nerves. I wonder what it must be like, knowing that ballet will go on for her after this. She's starting at LABT right after graduation.

I'm the opposite of Faye, exploding with anxiety. My whole life feels like it will be decided in one ten minute ballet. I'll have to go out there to be judged, do my best to be absolutely perfect, and still won't have control over anything. My stomach keeps turning over and I keep going to the bathroom to pee even though my bladder is empty.

When the stage manager calls five minutes, I put on my carefully broken-in pointe shoes and leave the dressing room to go down to warm up and watch the first part of the program from the wings. I can hear the rumble of the audience out in the house, and it generates a feeling of excitement backstage. The theater is filled with society's elite. Broadway producers, journalists and critics, wealthy patrons of the arts, movie stars, principal dancers from NBT and BNY, famous choreographers, and every major artistic director are in the audience. As I walk past people, I overhear everyone whispering about where Victor Caldwell, Charles Diamond, William Mason, and Bruce Pollock are sitting in the house.

The opening ballet is *Violins*, a classic Roizman piece set to Bach with eight women and one lead couple. I watch from the wings as I do my own warm-up. Faye, dressed in a black leotard and pink tights, and Jamal, in a white leotard and black tights, dance the *pas de deux*, moving slowly with grace. They look a little nervous, but it's a solid performance. They've had lots of rehearsals and their bodies move like machines.

Listening to the Bach Double Violin Concerto somehow lets me be okay with how the world is not exactly as I want it to be. I want to dance *Fire*, I want Victor Caldwell to pick me for BNY, and I want to fall in love. Maybe none of those things will happen, but there must be something greater than my disappointments if there's music this beautiful. The beauty of sound and movement is enough to make me feel there must be a God. My dad would be so proud of me just for thinking it.

Jeff Talroy appears backstage and stands in the front wing. His ballet, *Variations on a Theme,* begins with Jesse and six *corps de ballet* girls on stage. The girls wear blue leotards and short blue skirts, and Jesse wears a blue leotard and white tights. The curtain goes up and they're already in motion, their movements reflecting the music of Chopin. Jesse keeps glancing at Jeff Talroy in the front wing, as if to emphasize how much it means to him that Jeff chose him to dance his ballet. Sometimes I think that having someone believe that we can do something is all it takes to make us happy.

The ballet goes well, and after the first round of bows, Jesse runs to the wing and pulls Jeff Talroy onto the stage. I feel like they have an unusual connection, and great warmth towards each other. The audience goes wild, and at that moment I feel strongly that Jesse is going to make it. After the curtain falls, Jeff turns to Jesse and says, "Jesse, I had no idea you would look like that on stage. You danced it better than I even expected." I feel like Jeff's statement carries real weight, because I don't think that many people thought much of Jesse as a dancer before tonight. Jesse's lucky to have Jeff in his corner.

And sure enough, a moment later, Victor Caldwell appears backstage to offer Jesse an apprenticeship with BNY. I watch it happen, but I can't bring myself to feel that happy for him. I feel like it's a cruel joke. In the two years I've known Jesse, I never felt like he truly cared about getting in to BNY, and so even though I care about him it makes me mad.

Chapter 13

In a professional ballet company, they perform like this day in and day out. *I'd give anything to live my life like this all the time*, I think as I run back upstairs to take off my warm-ups and finish getting ready. My costume is a lavender romantic tutu, with rhinestones delicately embroidered on the bodice. The skirt comes just below my knees, and the elastic over my shoulders is skin-colored so the top looks strapless. I feel beautiful when I put it on and get a glimpse of myself in the mirror. There's no one around to hook me in, so I go downstairs with the back of my costume hanging open. Josie, one of the girls in the corps de ballet of *Violins*, is at the bottom of the stairs, and she kindly walks over and fastens the hooks for me.

I thank her and use the rest of intermission to try out some of my jumps and turns on the stage. I've learned the moments in *Waltz* when I can catch my breath, but I need to think about them before I go on. The first time we ran the entire ballet I was so spent by the end that it was all I could do to mark the steps. It's only in the last two weeks that I've had enough stamina to dance the whole thing full out.

"Places, please," the stage manager announces. Qi, in his usual quiet and sensitive way, leads me to the back wing. He's wearing a lavender tunic complementary to my tutu, with white tights, and he looks crisp and ready to go. The eight *corps de ballet* girls walk to a diagonal line on the stage and point their left toes in front of them. I can't help thinking that if I didn't know who they were, I wouldn't be able to tell them apart. They look identical with the same hairdos, the same pink costumes, and the same body types.

The orchestra begins to play the Glinka music, and I'm pleased to see Tyler, Jamal, Jesse, Nicole, and Hilary gather in the wings to watch. As the curtain rises, the girls plunge into the opening steps. I rub my hands together and take a deep breath. The friction feels good. I can't believe the moment is finally here. I've waited so long for this performance, and I'm so happy that at last I'll have my chance to shine.

"Ready?" Qi asks. He puts one hand on my waist and offers me the other. I put my hand in his, squeeze, and we run out onto the stage.

The stage lights are bright, shining right in my eyes as Qi leads me across the stage. We dance the short opening and then run off, both gasping for air. I bend over next to him to catch my breath, but there's almost no time before my next entrance.

I run around the wing and right back onto the stage. My lungs somehow relax and I plunge into my first solo, feeling good, really good. At the end I nail my *piqué arabesque* balance and the audience breaks into applause. I run off as Qi begins his solo.

My favorite part is my second variation, which is light and playful. I enter and take the opening pose as Qi runs into the wing. My mind focuses, I smile as I begin, and then it's all about being in the moment. I'm just *so happy.*

I've never performed for such an important audience. All the shows I did at home in Rock Island were mostly for family and friends. This audience is far more critical, even with my small family contingent out there for support. Even though it feels like I'm dancing just for myself, there are real people out there. I like that a dance meant for one person can reach hundreds.

Before I know it I'm racing through the finale, smiling, puffing, and trying desperately to feel my feet and push past the exhaustion. As the curtain falls and the audience breaks into applause, I leap into the wing and collapse. A second later, I'm up and taking my place onstage for the bow.

The curtain rises and Qi leads me forward to the audience. I can't believe how quickly it went—how can it be over already? I feel like I just started. I extend my right arm over my head and point my right foot behind me, knowing more than ever that dancing is a privilege. The applause seems to melt the past away. My right hand comes to my heart as I kneel, and I bow my head in a *grande révérance.*

Someone who sounds like my dad yells, "Bravo!" and I laugh and feel tears come to my eyes. Out of the corner of my eye, I see Tyler clapping wildly in the wing.

When the curtain comes down, Qi and I walk offstage together. Neither of us has fully recovered our breathing from the end of the ballet, but we're smiling. Vivienne and Madame Sivenko come running up.

"Very nice," says Madame Sivenko.

"Good job," says Vivienne.

Their eyes shower me with pride. Performing makes me happy, but that look in Vivienne's eyes means success. They know, more than anyone, how far I've come, and their approval means everything to me.

Tyler comes over, picks me up by the waist, and twirls me around. "You rock," he says. I feel so happy.

Victor Caldwell slips through the door that leads out to the house, and my stomach drops at the sight of him. This is my moment. Tyler backs away. I feel like maybe I'm getting in.

Madame Sivenko and Vivienne turn to look at him as he walks straight towards me, and it's obvious they think something is about to happen too.

"Wonderful performance of *Waltz*," Victor Caldwell says in my general direction. "There's someone I must speak to." He smiles, looking around.

I step forward, shivering, ready.

"Qi," Victor Caldwell says, turning to my partner. "May I have a moment?" He takes Qi's arm and leads him a few feet away from us, and I stand there, gaping, as Victor Caldwell makes someone else's dream come true.

Vivienne walks over and puts her hand on my shoulder. "You've worked very hard," she says. The tears rise up in my eyes. I turn to look up at her but she's already walked off.

I can't believe it. I'm not getting into Ballet New York. After everything I've put myself through, it was all for nothing. I was good tonight, I know I was—this is as good as I can be. But I'm not good enough to make my dreams come true. I'm not tall enough, and even when I gave everything I thought I could give, Victor Caldwell still didn't fall in love with me. I feel so helpless, and so sad. If this dream isn't going to happen for me, does my life have any meaning? I've pinned all of my hopes to something impossible. I feel like such a fool.

I make myself go up to the dressing room to take off my makeup and change out of my *Waltz* costume during the intermission. I feel like I'm in shock as I pull on jeans, a t-shirt, and sneakers. A few minutes ago I felt on top of the world, and now my life feels like it means nothing.

When I get back to the wings, the lights have already come up for *Fire* and the dancers are getting into their places. Tyler and Hilary are practicing the spin-away turn at the end of the *pas de deux*. He's wearing a ruby-studded tunic and white tights, and she matches him in a brilliant red ruby-covered leotard with a short paneled skirt. I stand back in the shadows, admiring them, but Tyler spots me and jogs over. He looks so handsome.

"Hey," he whispers, putting his arms around my waist. "Great job."

"Thanks," I say, but I can't look him in the eyes. I don't feel like he'll want to associate with me when he realizes I'm not getting into BNY.

"Kiss for good luck?" he asks.

I blink, surprised. He pecks me on the lips, and jogs back across the stage to find Hilary.

The music begins and the *corps de ballet* takes their places. The curtain goes up. The music and movement are riveting, but *Fire* floats by in front of my eyes, not fully registering. Tyler and Hilary run out onstage and the audience gasps. They're everything the audience expects to see at this performance—beautiful, young, and energetic—the future of ballet. Their dancing is strong and confident, but I can't help thinking that she's cold, and just the slightest bit uncoordinated. I know they don't have the connection that Tyler and I do when we dance. But the audience doesn't know that. The audience knows only what they see.

If I can want something so desperately, for so long, and then not only not get it, but realize it didn't matter so much, what does that mean? Marie didn't even come to the performance, and Jen is performing across the plaza at the Metropolitan Opera House tonight. Maybe dancing in front of an audience doesn't prove I'm worthy. I wonder if Nicole feels content tonight, sitting out in the audience. I can't imagine that she's happy either. She's never happy.

I watch Tyler and Hilary take their bows. She's radiant, basking in the light of her good fortune, with Tyler by her side. I'm so jealous I can hardly breathe. I hate myself for being so bitter, but I keep it together long enough to hug Tyler and tell him how wonderful he danced. Everyone pushes forward to congratulate him, so it's easy to slip away fast after he lets go of me. I feel relieved to walk out of the theater. My parents are waiting in front of the house for me after the show, holding hands. Dad's holding a bouquet of flowers.

"You were so beautiful, sweetie, so beautiful," Mom says. "I always knew you could do this." Her eyes tear up.

When she lets me go, Dad hands me the flowers and hugs me tight. He doesn't say anything, but I can tell from the look on his face and his body language that something has changed for him. For so long I felt like he never took my ballet dreams seriously, but tonight he seems to understand why I love dance, and how much it means to me.

We go out for a late dinner, and even though I'm heartbroken and exhausted, it's the most at ease the three of us have been together in years. I feel more relaxed spending time with them now, even though I still have one more performance left to get through.

"Did you like it?" I ask them as they walk me back to the dormitory. I feel like I need their approval.

"Like it? You were amazing," Dad says.

"We're so proud!" Mom says, clutching her program. They're both glowing, and it makes me feel happy.

"Seriously," Dad says. "We know you all can dance, and we know the choreography is great, but that's not what we came all the way here for, you know."

"What are you talking about? You came to see the best ballets in the world."

Dad puts a hand on my shoulder and we stop walking. He turns me to face him. "Anna," he says. "We came because we love you. You mean more to us than any performance ever could. Don't you realize what's so important about what you've achieved? It isn't getting into Ballet New York, or being better than the other girls. What matters is that you had a dream, and you fulfilled that dream. That's a rare thing. We're so proud of you."

Tears roll down my face and I reach up to wipe them away, embarrassed. "I'm so glad you came," I say.

"Oh honey," Mom says, "we are too. We wouldn't have missed this for the world."

"Thanks." I hug them both, feeling grateful.

"Goodnight," they say, and I wave before turning to walk into the building and press the button for the elevator. The lobby is silent. I take a deep breath and marvel at my life.

The elevator doors open, but before I get in, I glance outside. My parents are just two silhouettes, walking away from me into the night holding hands. I know they helped make me what I am, and that their love will protect me through whatever I'm meant to become.

Jen is back in the room when I get home, getting ready for bed after her own performance. "How did it go?" she asks. She crawls in bed, looking exhausted.

"It went," I say, wanting to open up to her like I used to, but feeling insecure. "The performance was fine. I'm so glad I have both of the shows tomorrow off. I have to be at the theater to cover, but it'll be an easy day. Then just one more performance Sunday, and it's all over." I sigh, realizing how fast everything seems to be flying by. I thought this weekend would never arrive, and now it's almost over. "How was *Swan Lake*?"

"Not too bad," she says. "I just haven't figured out how to stop my calves from cramping when we stand in that line through the whole *pas de deux*. But it's okay."

I feel like she's so lucky to be in *Swan Lake* with NBT. I can only imagine what it must be like. She seems like she's in a whole other world than me now.

"I have the matinee off on Sunday," Jen says, "so if I can get out at half hour I think I can slip away to see you dance your last performance of *Waltz*."

"Really?" I ask, amazed. "That's so nice. It's not that big a deal." Jen always manages to surprise me by how much she cares, and I feel a rush of appreciation for her.

"Well," she says, opening her eyes to look at me. "I wanted to cheer you on."

"Thanks, Jen." She's such a good friend. She never thinks about our differences, she always focuses on what we can share. I feel so lucky to have her in my life, not because of who she is as a dancer, but because she's such a good person. I feel like she makes *me* a better person.

I flip the light off and crawl into bed. "By the way, did you hear that Jesse and Qi got in to BNY today?" I ask.

"They did?" she asks in the darkness, and I hear a trace of regret in her voice. "I hadn't heard."

"Yeah," I say, and we bond over it without saying another word, even though she's already long past letting go of that dream.

Jen starts to snore lightly, and even though I'm exhausted, I lie awake in bed for a long time. The performances were over so fast. It felt so different from *Nutcracker,* or the other shows I used to dance in back home. In Rock Island, all it took to make me feel like a star was walking onstage and the sensing the approval of the audience, but real ballet demands a reach for perfection, not applause. I feel like performing here is about dancing the ballets as well as I possibly can, not about being the center of attention. I think I like it that way, despite how frequently overlooked I feel. If I work for myself and not for others, it makes me feel like no matter what I'm dancing, I'm doing something important.

On Saturday, I have a quick breakfast with my parents, take the warm-up class, and go over to the theater to sign in. I'm not performing today at all, which is kind of a relief. My parents decide to take the day to go to the Metropolitan Museum of Art, and go to the opera tonight, and I'm glad they're having a little vacation too, not just stuck at the theater with me the whole time. It's fun to hang out backstage and watch everyone, without having my own anxiety about performing.

Tyler is off during the matinee too, and we sneak out and sit in the audience together, like old times. Hilary and Charlie dance *Waltz*, and they're fine in it, even though she skipped so many rehearsals. It feels strange to watch Hilary dance it though, since I've come to think of it as my ballet. I wish Marie could have shared that part with me. When I saw Marie a few days ago in the cafeteria, she said she wasn't planning to come to the workshop performances at all.

When the lights go down for *Fire*, Tyler takes my hand. He's never done that before. Stravinsky's music starts quietly, the curtain goes up and the music is suddenly loud and energetic as the dancers stomp and flash across the stage, sharp and pristine in their red costumes. Nicole and Jamal run on, and I'm surprised at how good they look onstage. They're sexy and polished, and I can't help it, I love the ballet more than ever. I'm happy watching it, and even though Tyler and I aren't dancing it together, I know we feel the same love for it and that will have to be enough.

I leave Tyler to go off and meet my parents for dinner before the opera. My dad tries to bring up college during the meal, and I leave feeling frustrated and angry at them for trying to make me face reality. I don't want to think about reality, not this weekend, so I end up leaving the table before they've paid the bill. I kiss them goodbye and tell them I'll see them tomorrow, excusing myself.

As I'm crossing the plaza on the way back to the theater, I run into Vivienne and Simon, walking arm in arm.

"Hi, Anna," Vivienne says, pausing. She still looks like a ballerina, in tight blue leggings, a gauzy blouse, and jeweled flats. Simon is wearing a navy jacket and a bow-tie. He looks so elegant, and I take in his white hair and kind face with affection. I feel important just knowing them.

"Hi," I say, feeling warmly towards both of them. I feel like Vivienne taught me so many important lessons. She taught me how to fight for things, and when not to fight for things. I'm not as personally connected with Simon, but he taught me a great deal too. He showed me how to let my mind be quiet in order to know myself.

"Are your parents in town?" Vivienne asks, showing more interest in me as a person than she ever has before.

"Yes, thanks," I say, "I'm so glad they could be here."

"That's wonderful," Simon says.

"I'm so sad to be almost done," I say, mustering up my courage, "And Vivienne, I guess you were right when we talked last year. I probably will end up going to college, even after all of this."

She looks me over, and Simon squints, studying me closer. I feel more comfortable now with them than I ever have before, maybe because I don't have anything left to prove. I've done everything I can.

I'm surprised when Vivienne puts her hand on my shoulder and looks me right in the eye. "Anna," Vivienne says. "I can't predict the future. I don't know what's going to happen. But I do watch dancers every day," she says, and her mouth turns up in a smile. "I can tell everything about your personality by the way you dance. And I don't think it's over for you yet."

Simon reaches forward and squeezes my hand.

I nod, feeling my lower lip tremble. Vivienne holds my eyes for a moment before Simon nods back at me, drops my hand, and guides her away. As I watch them disappear into the crowd at Lincoln Center, I think they look so ethereal they could almost be mistaken for children. I feel deeply touched. I don't think they'll ever fully understand how much they've shaped my life.

The evening performance is uneventful, and I'm restless and eager to go home and get to bed. I've started to feel anxious about tomorrow. Hanging out and watching everyone else perform starts to lose appeal. I sit backstage and put a hand against my forehead. My skin feels warm, I'm sweating a lot, and I wonder if I'm getting sick. Dancers rush past me in their costumes, excited and bubbling with energy while I feel irritated and anxious for the show to be over. As soon as the curtain goes up on *Fire*, I stand up and slip out the back door. I'm sure no one will notice if I don't stay until the end.

I walk back to the dorm. Jen is snoring softly in our room. I fall into bed, exhausted. I'm asleep before my head reaches the pillow.

Jen is gone when I wake up, feeling sick. My forehead is burning up and I can't get out of bed. I'm already almost late for the warm-up class, and it starts in less than an hour. I can't believe today's matinee is the last workshop performance. I feel sad that this could be the last time I'll ever get to perform *Waltz*.

I take three aspirin and go to the studio. Everyone is excited to be so close to being done, and even if I'm coming down with something, I have to get through it. I feel horrible, but I tell myself over and over that I'm fine. I'm fine.

Madame Sivenko comes in, claps her hands, and gestures to the pianist. We start *barre*. I *plié* and force myself to focus on the familiar movements. My body feels shaky and weak, and the more I dance the worse I start to feel. Usually if I don't feel great before class, dancing makes me feel better. Today it makes me feel worse.

I stand in the back during center, sure I'm running a fever. I feel as if I might pass out if I let go of the *barre*.

"Are you all right?" Hilary asks with concern in her voice. It unnerves me even more that she's the one taking notice. I must look horrible.

"I've felt better," I admit, immediately feeling upset that I give this to her. Just looking at Hilary brings up years of anger and resentment inside of me.

Hilary nods and walks forward to dance, and I wonder if she gets as much satisfaction out of my suffering as it seems like she does. How could anyone be like that? I do my best to pull it together and finish the class, but I dance poorly. At least no one seems to be paying close attention. Today hardly seems like a day that matters. The year is over. Madame Sivenko isn't even bothering to correct us, and she hardly seems to be watching. When she seems to be looking at the other side of the room I stop and mark some of the combinations, trying to conserve my energy.

But when the class ends, Madame Sivenko comes right over to me, and I realize I was stupid to think she wouldn't notice I'd been slacking off. She notices everything. "Anna, you look terrible," she says. "You barely danced today." She touches my forehead. "You're burning up."

I cringe, feeling ashamed. She always seems to see exactly what we want to hide. I feel like Madame Sivenko would never come over to me after class if I'd danced well. I've spent the last two years believing we were never allowed to be sick.

"I'm okay," I reply. I tell myself that no fever is going to wreck my last chance to get onstage.

"You look ill," Madame Sivenko persists. I feel like she's spent years teaching me never to have a problem that people can see, and feel frustrated that now she's the one making this an issue.

"I'm just a little rundown, but I'll be fine today," I insist. Hilary lingers a few feet away.

"There's no need to be a hero," Madame Sivenko says, crossing her arms and appraising me from head to toe.

"I said I'm fine," I say, picking up my bag. "I need to get over to the theater."

""Well then," Madame Sivenko says. I hurry past her and Hilary out the door.

On my way over to the theater I get the chills, and I'm frustrated that I feel even worse. I still don't have a job, any job. I know some of the directors are still here. There's no way I'm not going to perform, but all I want to do is go lie down.

I put on my makeup and get dressed in a daze. I hardly hear people talking to me in the dressing room and my head continues to throb. As much as I hate to admit it, I feel awful.

As soon as I'm ready, I go to a dark corner backstage to stretch. Tyler comes down the stairs and grabs onto a boom near me to do his own warm-up for *Violins*. He catches my eye. We nod at each other and then go back to our own preparations.

The dancers in *Violins* gather onstage, practicing and whispering. I can hear the audience talking in the house. Even after three shows, I can still feel everyone's excitement and anticipation. The lights go down, the curtain goes up, and the Bach Double Violin Concerto begins. I walk into the third wing to watch. My classmates are out there, dancing their hearts out.

Hilary walks up next to me in the wing, wearing jeans and a t-shirt. "You still look sick," she whispers. "Maybe I should dance *Waltz*."

"I'm fine," I say firmly. I grip the boom so tightly my knuckles turn white. This one performance seems like everything to me. It might be the last performance I ever get.

"You don't look fine," Hilary says, breathing down my neck.

I spin around to face her. "I said I'm fine."

Hilary laughs. "Whatever you say."

"You can't buy your way into all of my performances," I say. "Back off."

"What did you say?" she asks, her pretend lightheartedness gone in an instant. "Just what do you think you're implying?" Her eyes flash a warning at me.

But I'm at the end of my patience with her. I'm done. "You heard me. This is my performance, and I'd appreciate it if you'd get the hell away from me."

She grabs my wrist and pulls my face up next to hers, shocking me. "You're asking for it, bitch," she says. "I was trying to help you." She spits the word *help* in my face.

"You little—" I start, but Tyler is suddenly there, pulling us apart.

"Stop it, you two," he says, pulling Hilary back and stepping in between us. "Don't do this."

"But she——" I start. He puts a finger to my lips.

"I was just trying to help," Hilary says sweetly. "Anna's sick today and I was nice enough to offer to cover for her."

Tyler looks at me. "Are you sick?" he asks.

I look away from him. He puts his hand to my forehead, and I flinch.

"Wow, babe," he says, "you're running a fever."

I let out a sigh.

"Look," he says, "maybe it wouldn't hurt for Hilary to put on the other costume and stand in the wings."

"That's what I thought," she says. She turns triumphantly and walks off towards the dressing rooms.

I close my eyes and breathe. It seems like everything is happening too fast. I feel so out of control.

"I'm sorry, Anna," Tyler says. "I didn't mean to take Hilary's side. You're really warm. Do you feel like you can dance?"

"I have to dance," I say, pushing past him. "Leave me alone."

The final movement of *Violins* starts. I walk back to the alcove behind the stage to get a drink from the water fountain. Everything is dark in the back, but I know where to go without the lights. I drink and drink until I can barely breathe. I'm afraid my mouth will go dry when I start dancing. When I come up for air cold rushes to my head and I stagger away from the fountain. There's a small private bathroom back here that no one ever uses, but I lurch towards it, feeling like I'm going to vomit. I can hear the music speeding up as *Violins* is about to end, and I know I don't have much time before *Waltz*.

I jiggle the door handle to the bathroom and at first it sticks, but when I shake it again it swings open. I blink, the nausea momentarily forgotten when my eyes adjust to the light.

"Oh my God," I say.

And there is Jeff Talroy and Jesse, together in the bathroom, locked in a passionate embrace.

A million questions run through my mind before they even stop to look at me. Why would Jeff Talroy have an affair with a student? Did Jesse kissing me mean anything at all? Did Jesse see this as a way to get in to BNY, and was it?

I slam the door shut as Jesse starts to say my name. I hurry back to the stage. It's time to go on.

When the curtain comes down after *Violins*, I walk onstage to try out a few steps during the intermission. My mind is spinning. Qi walks up next to me. "Should we try a lift?" he asks with concern. He's always so considerate.

"I'm not feeling very good, just so you know."

He touches my cheek. "Hot. No good."

"Let's try the fish dive." I say, trying to smile.

"Okay," he says. He walks downstage and waits. I'm supposed to run and leap into his arms. The corps girls are practicing around us.

My mind goes blank. "Qi," I say. "I've forgotten the entire ballet."

"Ha ha," Qi says. He looks nervous but he smiles. "Impossible. We rehearse *Waltz* for two months."

But for the life of me I can't think of the choreography. It will just have to come back when I hear the music. I figure that we practice so much so our bodies will automatically know what to do. If I ever needed my muscle memory, now is the time.

Qi shrugs and walks over to the side to rub rosin into his hands, which slipped on my waist a little in the *promenade* last night. The rosin will make his hands stick to the satin on my costume. I follow him into the wing as the Glinka music begins. He puts one hand on my waist and offers me the other. The *corps de ballet* begins to dance and the curtain goes up. I squeeze Qi's hand. We run onto the stage.

The lights are bright, and they disorient me as we make our entrance. Jamal appears in the front wing wearing his *Fire* costume, glowing red behind the stage lights. Hilary walks up behind him wearing an identical costume to the one I have on.

Qi lifts me across the stage, puts me down gently, and we continue the ballet. I dance the best that I can, even though I don't feel well. At the end of the opening Qi guides me off into the wing.

"Good," Qi says, putting his hands on his knees and leaning over to breathe. We both are always gasping for air by this point, but today is the worst it's ever been. I bend over next to him to catch my breath and can't seem to get air back into my lungs.

The ballet continues, and onstage the *corps de ballet* moves from pattern to pattern. I run around the wing and back onto the stage for my first solo. The girls clear as I tear across the stage, my feet racing through the footwork on autopilot. I can hardly feel my body, and I can't help thinking dancers are such a contradiction, because no matter how much we love to dance, we're out here leaping and smiling while our feet are bleeding and our hearts are breaking. Sometimes I wonder what I'm doing to myself.

I break into a smile when I see the three people standing the front wing on the other side of stage from Jamal and Hilary. Jen, Marie, and Tyler have appeared out of nowhere, gathered there together. They smile back at me and I feel a rush of happiness.

I feel inspired that my best friends in the world are here, despite everything. I tune into how beautiful the music is, and for a few minutes, the stage is mine, the audience is mine, and the performance itself is mine. My conscious mind focuses on the choreography and the moment alone, but there's a deeper part of me that comes out, a part that Simon would be proud of. I feel like I fully express who I *am*.

At the end of the variation I whip out a final double turn. On the last note of the music, I step forward towards my friends' wing on my right toe and lift my left leg high behind me. My right arm stretches in front of my chest. As I look over my extended right fingers, my left arm reaches back parallel to my left leg. I can feel the music through every inch of my body.

The audience breaks into applause. I come off pointe and walk forward to bow, but I'm so dizzy. I scan the audience trying to steady myself, but it's too dark to see anyone. The lights are very bright and I almost pitch forward into the orchestra pit. The clapping dies down as I turn and run into the wing.

I reach towards Jen, Marie, and Tyler, stumbling, my legs buckling beneath me. The orchestra picks up the music and continues. They reach forward to catch me as the world goes black.

Chapter 14

The next thing I hear is applause.

Jen presses a wet towel to my face. I reach up to push her hand away, thinking that my makeup will be ruined. "Are you okay?" she asks.

"I'm so happy you're all here," I say. "Marie, it means so much to me that you came. I know you didn't want to come."

"Of course I would not miss your big performance," Marie says, hovering next to Jen.

"What happened?" I'm lying on the floor backstage. "Why did the music stop?"

"*Waltz* is over," Jen says.

"Over?" I ask, sitting up to look at the stage. "Oh my God." Qi is leading Hilary forward to bow in front of the line of corps girls. Applause pours out of the house.

"You fainted and Hilary went on for you," Tyler says from behind Jen and Marie. "She was ready in the wing." I feel a rush of frustration, and I scramble to my feet, feeling like my life must be over.

"Anna," Tyler says, fumbling over his words, "I didn't mean—"

"Oh my God," I say, ignoring him, "I have to get out of here. Tyler, go away."

"But I lo—" he starts.

"I said, go away," I insist, turning away from his crestfallen expression.

"Let me help you," Jen says, following me as I stumble towards the crossover. "Are you going to be okay?" Marie asks, right behind us. Jen grabs my arm as I stumble along the narrow passageway behind the backdrop. They exchange a look of concern.

"Just get me to the dressing room to get my stuff," I say. I'm still dizzy and nauseous. I've never been so humiliated. Jen yanks on my arm to stop me from falling when I trip over a wire.

It's a relief to find the dressing room deserted. "Don't cry yet," Jen says, watching me.

I rip my costume off and yank out my headpiece. Jen sweeps all my makeup and hair things into a bag while I throw my sweat suit on. I'm trying to stay in control, but the tears start and I can't stop them. "I can't believe this happened," I sob.

"Tyler said you are sick," Marie says, her voice full of sympathy. "He was worried about you."

"It's no excuse," I say sharply. "And what does Tyler care, anyway?"

"I think he cares a lot," Marie says, but I don't want to think about it now.

Jen takes my hand and leads me down the stairs. Marie follows us, carrying my bag I hurry them through the door to the lobby, feeling a rising sense of terror at the sound of Vivienne's shoes clicking down the hall towards us. Vivienne is the last person I want to see. I feel like I've let everyone down.

My parents are the only people standing in the lobby. I can hear Stravinsky's *Capriccio* behind the closed doors to the house, and push away the thought of Jamal and Nicole out on the stage dancing *Fire*.

"What happened?" Mom asks, her voice full of worry. "One minute she was dancing, and then halfway through the ballet another girl ran on in her costume."

"She has a fever. She passed out in the wings," Jen explains.

"It was very dramatic," Marie adds.

They introduce themselves, but even though I've told my parents so much about my friends, I can't bring myself to participate in small talk right now. I feel myself pulling away from the present moment, and my mind wanders back to right before I fainted. If only I had pushed a little harder. If only I hadn't been so weak.

Marie excuses herself to sneak back into the theater and watch Jamal.

I give her a sad wave. "Thanks for coming," I say, feeling ashamed. She smiles and shrugs.

"I'll see you later, Anna," Jen says. "I have to go back to work." She gives me a hug before slipping out the door. I wish she hadn't come. Now she'll always think of me this way, and I'm afraid she'll never respect me as a dancer.

My parents walk me back to the dorms, and their presence comforts me. "Did you see *The New York Times* review this morning?" Mom asks me. "You had a picture and a nice mention!"

"They called you 'piquant,'" Dad adds. He elbows me, trying for a smile, but I can't be happy right now. At least the critics didn't see today's performance. They don't praise dancers who pass out in the middle of their own performance.

The dorms are deserted when we get back. I see my reflection in the mirror and it's monstrous: tears running down my cheeks, hair falling out of the bun, makeup streaked across my face. I unpin my hair.

"Do you want us to stay?" Mom asks, wanting to fix the situation but only irritating me by trying. I shake my head. Dad puts his hand on her arm as if to say they should let it be.

"Okay, sweetie, feel better," she says as they turn off the light. They both kiss me on the cheek before slipping out the door.

When I'm alone I cry my eyes out, until my head feels like it's going to explode. There's no way I'll get in anywhere now.

I dream of Stacy Hannah twirling off into the glare of the stage lights. I'm running after her, my bun falling out, my tutu ripped. "Stacy!" I scream and scream, but I can't see her face, and she doesn't stop.

The phone wakes me up. Every muscle in my body aches. It rings and rings and finally falls silent. I think of all the years I planned to be a dancer, and how it all amounted to nothing. I've never felt so lost.

And then it starts to ring again.

I'm still half-asleep, but I walk out into the hall to pick it up. "Hello?"

"Anna, this is Madame Sivenko." My stomach drops. "Come down to my office immediately."

I dread the thought of it. "I can't, I'm sick," I say.

"This isn't a request," she says firmly. "Five minutes." The receiver clicks.

I walk over to the mirror, wondering how to proceed in this situation. For a moment I just stand there, staring at myself, terror rising in my chest.

I muster up all the energy I can and walk to the elevator and ride down to the fifth floor. I'm so scared I start to hyperventilate.

The hall smells like Simon's pipe when I get off the elevator, a sign the teachers are in a conference. There's a small crowd standing by the front desk. I recognize Nicole's mom, hugging an elderly woman. I guess the group must be Nicole's family, because I see Nicole right in the center, tears streaming down her face.

"Ballet New York," Nicole's mom says to no one in particular. "My daughter, an apprentice with Ballet New York. I'm so proud." She turns to another man and starts hugging him. They're all hugging, and jumping up and down. I feel strange being miserable in the face of so much joy.

I slip past and round the corner, crashing right into Hilary as she comes charging down the hall. She plows right into me.

"Watch it," she says. She pauses, and I'm taken by how uncharacteristically happy she seems too. "Oh, and you're welcome," she says.

"Yeah," I say.

"Want to hear my big news?" she asks.

I shake my head and keep walking. She lets me go. I can't take any more big news.

I walk into the foyer in front of Madame Sivenko's office. She's behind her desk, talking to others, fiddling with her diamond necklace. Simon is hunched over his pipe, sitting next to the door. Vivienne is sitting next to him with her legs and arms crossed. They make me feel so intimidated.

"...learned *Fire*—" Vivienne is saying. She snaps her mouth shut the second she sees me in the doorway.

"I can wait outside." I'd prefer to be anywhere else but here.

"No, come in, Anna," Madame Sivenko says, standing up. Simon puffs away on his pipe.

I continue lingering in the doorway. "I'm sorry about the performance. I had a fever."

"We know you were sick," Vivienne says, and her voice is friendly, confusing me because the teachers are never understanding about illness or injury. Sick means the same thing as lazy here. I prepare for the worst.

Madame Sivenko walks around the desk. "Come in the office, Anna," she says. "Have a seat. We'll leave you two alone."

I step forward into the office at the same time a man with silver hair stands up from the chair on the inside of the doorway. William Mason is not that tall, about sixty years old, with a strong jaw and piercing eyes. Even though we've never met, I've been studying pictures of him since I was a little girl.

"Thanks Natasha," he says. His voice is commanding but soft. "We'll just be a few minutes."

The shock of it begins to register as Madame Sivenko, Simon, and Vivienne walk out of the room. Vivienne squeezes my arm as she passes me.

"I enjoyed your performances this weekend," he says, offering me his hand. All I can think of is the rejection letter from LABT.

"I'm sorry, I've been sick." I take a step backward instead of shaking his hand, feeling shy.

"I heard," he says, lowering his hand. "Could we sit for a minute?" He gestures to a chair and we sit down across from each other.

I have no idea what to say.

"Stacy Hannah is a big fan of yours," he says. He's charming and charismatic, and I feel drawn to him immediately.

I finally find my voice. "Me?"

He nods. "I'd like to offer you an apprenticeship with my ballet company," he says.

Somehow I manage not to cry. Instead I nod and listen while he tells me information I already know: that LABT has forty-five dancers, dances Roizman ballets as well as new works by resident choreographer Simone Reese, and in the fifteen years since its inception has already become one of the top five companies in the United States.

"The contract is thirty-five weeks," he says, "We need you to start as soon as possible."

I feel overwhelmed.

"Here's my card," he says. "Please let me know in the next day or two if you'll be joining us."

"Okay," I manage. "Thank you."

"You can also call the company manager, George," he says. "He can help you with further questions. We'll overnight your contract, and you'll need to sign and return it by the end of the week." He stands up.

I nod and stand too. Can my life really change this fast?

His eyes study me intently and he smiles. "I'm looking forward to working with you," he says, and I feel like a whole new world has just opened for me.

Vivienne is waiting for me by the elevator when I walk out of the meeting with William. "Congratulations!" she says. I'm surprised and touched when she gives me a hug. "Did you accept?"

"I...I told him I needed to think about it."

"You should take the contract," Vivienne says. "William's a legend, and his company is doing so well, already in the top five. This is a real job, what you wanted." She lifts my chin to make me look her in the eye.

"I know," I say. "I can't believe it!"

"Believe it," she says.

"Can I ask you a question, even if it's a stupid one?" I ask.

She raises her eyebrow.

"Did I ever have a chance at BNY?" I ask.

"Take the job, Anna," she says, falling back into her usual practical manner, and I feel silly for even asking. "Don't be a fool. Most of your classmates aren't getting one, and this is the top school in the country."

"I know." My voice comes out in a whisper, and I realize I don't know what I'm supposed to feel, not after I've waited for an opportunity like this my whole life, and now it's here. I'm so grateful. I get in the elevator, trying to comprehend that something really good has finally happened to me. My eyes meet Vivienne's one last time, right before the door shuts, and I can see she's happy for me too.

Chapter 15

I call my parents at their hotel.

"What's going on?" Mom asks. "How are you feeling?"

"Still sick, but it's not important. I got a job. Mom, *I got a job.*"

"What?" Dad says. "What are you talking about?"

That's when it hits me how happy I feel. Overjoyed. Overwhelmed. Amazed. "I made it! William Mason offered me a job with Los Angeles Ballet Theatre." Just saying the words fills my heart with elation, and the promise of so much yet to come.

"You're kidding," Mom says, but she sounds giddy. "Really?"

"Fainting and all?" Dad asks, chuckling.

"Really," I say. "Really really really." I feel so happy. In fact, I feel like the luckiest girl in the world. This might be the best day of my entire life.

On my way home from the celebration dinner with my parents, I see Tyler walking out of the dorm with his mom. She seems distant and stern, with short gray hair and a serious face, but he grabs her arm and pulls her towards me.

"Anna," he says, "Is it true about LABT?"

I grin. "It's true," I say. "How did you hear? Is this your mom?" I turn and offer her my hand.

"I've heard so much about you," she says, and I feel like I was wrong to judge her so quickly. Her voice is warm and caring, and she clasps my hand between both of her own. We smile at each other.

"Congratulations," Tyler says. "I'm so happy for you."

"Thanks," I say. "I can't believe it."

"I can," he says softly. His mom puts her arm around his shoulder, as if to signal she wants to protect him. "I just can't believe you're moving to California," he says. He shrugs her arm away, and she steps back.

"I'm sort of in denial," I say.

"It's very exciting news," Tyler's mom says.

"I always thought I wanted to get into BNY," I say. "But I'm not tall enough, and this is going to be much better for me. It's kind of a dream come true—a dream I didn't even know I had. Life is surprising these days."

"Yeah," Tyler says, staring at me, and we hold each other's gaze for a long moment. I wave goodbye and walk past them into the building, feeling like my heart might break at the thought that I'm moving across the country from him.

I call the number on William Mason's business card. His secretary says he's in rehearsal, and she puts me on to George Summers, the company manager. I accept the job offer, and at eighteen years old, I become a professional dancer.

"Welcome to the Los Angeles Ballet Theatre," George says, at the end of the call.

"Thanks," I say.

"And I'm sure you're happy to have your friends Faye and Hilary coming with you," he adds.

"What?" I ask, shocked. I was excited knowing that Faye would be going too, but it hadn't even occurred to me that Hilary must have met with William Mason right before I did. I can't decide if I feel relieved that she didn't get into BNY either, or horrified at the thought of us in the same company.

The contract and season schedule comes overnight, and I sign on the dotted line. Hilary or no Hilary, William Mason picked me, and it's going to work out.

On Wednesday morning, I Fedex the contract back to Los Angeles. LABT is a non-union company that follows union regulations. I won't be joining the dancer's union like Jen did, but I'll have a weekly salary, health insurance, and a retirement fund. My mom takes me to get my passport, which I'll need if we tour abroad. The upcoming season only has domestic tours on the schedule, but the company goes to Europe occasionally. My mom is already studying up on all the things I'll need to think about and plan for, but I'm still caught up in graduation and packing up and leaving New York. My graduation ceremony flies by, but I'm especially happy to have earned a real high school diploma. Everything seems to be coming together.

Dad goes back to Rock Island the morning after I graduate from YAH. "I'm sorry I can't go with you and Mom to LA," he says as Mom hails him a cab. "Work calls." He gives me a warm hug and then he's gone.

It's going to be a long time before I can go home again, but I feel ready for whatever lays ahead.

I call Rachel in Rock Island to tell her my news. She's been busy competing in horse shows and in love with her latest boyfriend.

"Your parents aren't making you go to college?" she asks. I picture her face that I've known for so long, giving me the same old look of surprise. If I thought I didn't fit with kids my age before, I certainly don't fit in with them now. "I'm going to Northwestern next fall," she says.

"If I'm going to do this, now is the time," I tell her.

"Yeah," she says. "I just feel like you're missing out on so much."

"I know," I say. "But I can't pass up this opportunity."

"True," she says. "I could never do what you're doing."

"Honestly, Rach," I say, "I don't think I know how to do anything else."

Jen moves out of the dorm into her own apartment. I help her carry bags of stuff up Columbus

Avenue. It's so sad to see her half of the room bare. We sit on the wood floor of her unfurnished studio and eat pizza, silent. It feels like a death, after living together for two years, even though we're both excited about the future.

"Hilary actually said congratulations to me in the cafeteria this morning," I tell her.

"That's wild," Jen says. "Maybe you'll end up friends in LA." She hands me a Coke as we both roll our eyes. It makes me smile. "Any regrets about the other companies?" she asks.

"What's the point? I don't like to regret things. LABT is going to be great." But of course there's regret. If only I was taller maybe I would have had a shot at BNY. I think about how crazy it is that we're never really satisfied or happy as dancers unless we're killing ourselves.

She laughs. "I bet someday you'll dance the lead in *Fire* with LABT," she says.

"Maybe. And you'll dance Giselle with NBT!"

"That sounds good," she agrees.

I look out the window at the city lights. I'm going to miss New York so much.

We hug each other tightly before Jen walks me out to the elevator. I think of the first time we hugged on the plaza a year and a half ago. "I'll miss you," we say at the same time. I laugh as I walk into the elevator.

"Why do we never end up dancing in the same place?" she asks. But the truth is, it's better this way—I'm glad we'll never have to compete.

"I feel like we went through the army together," I say.

"We did, in a way," Jen says, wiping her eyes.

The elevator opens and we hug. I watch the doors close on her.

I stop at the edge of the fountain at Lincoln Center on my way back to the dorm. I dig a penny out of my purse and toss it into the water, closing my eyes to make a wish.

When I lean over and check to see where it went, I see hundreds of pennies at the bottom. I say a prayer that wishes don't drown. What happened to all those wishes?

Faye and I ride every roller coaster at Six Flags on the SBNY end-of-the-year trip.

We climb into the teacups right before the park closes. Tyler, Jesse, and Jamal climb in a teacup across from us, just as Faye spins the wheel.

The ride begins. We spin away. Amusement park. Tyler. Screaming kids. Amusement park. Tyler. Screaming kids. Amusement park. Tyler.

I'm standing before the ride is even over, needing to get out. I take off running down the asphalt, not sure what I'm doing, just desperate to get away from myself. Faye runs after me. "Hey," she says. "What's the rush?"

"Sorry." I stop next to a tree and turn to face her. My eyes fill with tears, but I start to laugh too. "Why doesn't anything work out the way we want it to?"

"Maybe it does," she says, "and we just don't understand what we truly wanted until much, much later."

I'm lying awake in the middle of the night, unable to sleep my last night in the dorms. It seems so empty without Jen. The lights from Lincoln Center pour in through the window and illuminate the room.

There's a soft knock on the door.

"Who is it?" I ask. But I know who it is.

"Tyler."

"It's the middle of the night." I look down at my tank top and pajama pants.

"Are you asleep?" he asks, his voice muffled through the door.

I get up to let him in. He's standing there in his pajama pants and a white t-shirt, his hair rumpled.

"No," I say. "Can't sleep."

"Me either," he says. "May I come in?"

"Okay."

He walks in and climbs up on the bed. I close the door and get on the bed, sitting Indian style, facing him. We look at each other for a while and say nothing.

Finally I manage, "Did you know Jesse was gay?"

He smiles a little. "Did he tell you?"

"Not in so many words," I say.

"I can't believe you liked him," he says.

"I never liked him! Not that way."

"He made a pass at me at the beginning of the year," Tyler says. "I told him I wasn't gay and that I liked you. He got angry and insisted he wasn't gay either, but then he started bothering you. Now I hear he has something going with Jeff Talroy? Total scandal. He's still my friend though. I think he's confused."

I can't believe Tyler and Jesse talked about me so long ago and I didn't know.

"Hold it," I say. "Did you just say you liked me?"

He starts to climb off the bed.

"Hey, wait." I reach out and grab his hand. "Come back." I lay down on the bed, pulling him towards me. He waits for a moment, looking at me, and then he climbs in bed and we're kissing at last, gently at first, then harder, passionately. I run my fingers through his hair, kiss his cheeks, his earlobes, his neck. He cradles my head in his hands and I can feel his heart beating like crazy. His fingers run down this inside of my arm, stroking the inner part of my elbow.

We kiss like that for hours, caring for each other, being together.

After a while, I curl up into him and we fall sound asleep, wrapped in each other's arms.

He's gone when I wake up. I feel relieved not to have to say goodbye because I care too much.

I take a shower and put the rest of my things in my suitcase. My mom is waiting in the lobby. "Come on," she says, and I can see she's excited too. "Today's a big day." We hail a taxi to take us to JFK airport.

I watch the skyscrapers fade away as we leave the city behind. I feel like I've come so far since I came to New York two years ago. It's hard to believe I'm about to start my career with William Mason and Los Angeles Ballet Theatre, but I know I've earned it. I picture myself in my lavender *Waltz* tutu, a million tiny rhinestones in my hair, bowing my head in a *grand révérance* to this chapter in my life. I'm grateful this isn't the end. I feel like I'm just at the beginning.

Made in the USA
Lexington, KY
09 May 2013